SHE WENT LOOKING FOR LOVE

LANCE JONES

Dedication

Dedicated to my dear friends Lorna Wynter-Philp and Caroline Joseph, who continually encouraged me to write.

Acknowledgments

I want to thank God, for allowing me to accomplish a task that He laid on my heart and which became quite an enjoyable experience when I put pen to paper.

My thanks also go out to my beloved wife; the wife of my youth. She is a woman who loves me, cares for me and warmly encourages me.

My mother, Rachel Jones. She has been a great source of strength who offers continued support. She is a woman that always puts others first.

My children. You are all a true blessing.

To my brothers and sisters, my extended family and to my church family. I count it an honour that I have been called to serve you all.

Thank you, Anne-Marie Brown, Carleen Bennet and Norma Jones for stepping in right on time. May God truly bless you for that.

Contents

■ Foreword

Author, Lance G. Jones has written a compelling romantic/drama that reveals a deep understanding of human nature. The desire to love and be loved sometimes clashes with the reality of a world that doesn't operate according to script. The characters are so real you will think you know them. Their ups and downs, triumphs and failures will ring true in a way that you can't help but relate.

This book is anything but a tired re-telling of boy meets girl and lives happily ever after. While it has the sensitivity of deep love and true feelings, it does not shy away from the difficulties all relationships face. By doing that, the story rings true. You can't help but root for the protagonist, while also seeing the reality of flawed and sometimes evil people.

Once you are into the arc of the story, you will not want to stop reading until you see how it all ends. I couldn't put it down.

Nick Gugliotti
Author/Editor
CEO of C2 Consulting

1

◾ A Time of Innocence

We were a happy family the Bryans; my mother, father, older brother Richard and me, Jason.

"Why wouldn't we be happy?"

Mum and Dad loved each other deeply, in my home, there wasn't any lack of love. We were always laughing and joking together. One thing my father always insisted on, was that we all sat together, around the dining, table and ate together every evening. The dining table was the place where we all shared our stories and experiences. The place where my parents took us back into the past to share memories and stories of their upbringing; tales which taught me a lot about family and family-values that still remain with me to this day. It was the place where all the dots were joined together and where we got to know about our heritage and the generations that went before us.

Don't get me wrong, my brother and I would fight now and again, as all kids do but our quarrels were always over as quickly as they had begun. As a family we wanted for nothing. I'm not saying we were super-rich or anything, but my dad had a good job and we lived in a pleasant neighbourhood, what some people would call "a nice area." It was a cross between living in the countryside and yet we were a stone's throw away from town. We lived in what I would describe as a massive house with bathrooms everywhere. The garden was the size of a football pitch, well-kept with beautiful landscaping and perfectly placed garden furniture. For two boys, we had all the room to play all the games we could ask for. Mum and dad took us on luxurious holidays abroad each year and regularly took us out to nice restaurants. When I look back, I can say that I had a good start to life.

If I remember correctly, I was about seven years old when I first noticed that my mum seemed to look worried a lot of the time. Most days, when she brought my brother and I home from school, she seemed to be anxious, worried and concerned. She would often holler at us for charging around the house shouting our heads off.

"Shush, your father's asleep!" she would say, her anxiety etched in the lines at the corners of her eyes.

Not fully understanding why, we thought it had something to do with the fact that dad was always in bed and hardly ventured out of their bedroom. When we were curious as to why he was so often in bed at 4 o'clock in the afternoon, she would reply, "he was a bit under the weather at the moment." That "moment" seemed to go on for an awful long time. Sometimes we would peep around the bedroom door and if my dad was awake, he would smile lovingly at us, ask what we had been up to and want to know if we were alright. Despite this, he always seemed too tired to speak for long durations of time. Then one day, mum sat my brother and I down and said that dad had to go into hospital.

"Why?" we asked.

"To have some treatment," she said.

"Will he be better then?" my mum sort of nodded then got up quickly and left the room.

My dad must have been in the hospital for only a few days when my mum sat us down again. Her eyes were blood-shot and red, her face was sort of crumpled. When she spoke, her voice was cracked and hollow, "Boys," she said, "daddy has gone to be with the Lord."

"What do you mean gone to be with the Lord, is he coming back?" I asked.

"Shut up you idiot," my brother Richard shouted at me.

When you are young, the death of a parent can be as hard to understand as it is to bear. My dad had been an absolute rock-solid part of my world, he had just been so naturally there. And now he wasn't, it was almost impossible to accept – he can't just go like that. He can't just simply stop being there, it's impossible! Dad's don't just disappear like that.

With mum saying that he was "with the Lord" gave me little comfort. I was full of jealousy, anger; outraged that my dad would make the choice to be with the Lord and not with us where he belonged. It was a very difficult time for me, because there I was a little boy with lots of unanswered questions. It was so bewildering, this shattering thing that had happened to our happy family and I was supposed to accept it as God's purpose, it had no rhyme or reason. From the stability of our life together, it felt like I had been set adrift on a vast and empty ocean of uncertainty and bewilderment and there was no sign of land, no place of safety. It was like being punished at school for something you knew you couldn't possibly have done, only a billion times worse. If God truly loved and cared for us, why, why, why had he taken my dad away?

At the funeral, the Reverend said that some people's time to leave this earthly world and go to heaven, comes early and that although it made us all sad, it was for a purpose. Again, I asked myself, "what purpose?"

At first my brother Richard seemed to be more thoughtful than upset. Being five years older than me, I guess the reality of our dad's absence had sunk in more quickly for him. As we were to discover though, for him the effects would come later, like the aftershock of an earthquake.

"We must pray," my mum said, "always remember the power of prayer." How could she be so strong, and continue to believe, it was incredible. But lying in bed at night I would hear her crying quietly and I realized that beneath that strong personae she presented to the world each day, she too was adrift and was struggling to keep her faith.

2

Amanda Arrives

It was about a year later that Amanda came into my life. She moved into the big detached house a few doors away.

I saw her the day she arrived that sunny Saturday morning in springtime. She was sitting on the front steps of her new home, singing as the removal men carried in the furniture. I walked up to where she was sitting on the step and just stared at her. I was drawn to her as if by a magnet. She looked about the same age as me, about eight years old. I couldn't help but notice that her smooth skin was the colour of coffee. Cradled in her lap were two beautiful little dolls. With a small plastic brush, she was brushing their hair lovingly as she sang. Feeling very bold I asked her, "what are you singing?" The song was beautiful, and she had a lovely, sweet voice.

She broke off from what she was doing and looked up. I was startled to see that the colour of her eyes was emerald green. With these remarkable, piercing eyes she carried on looking at me for several seconds before replying, "Amazing Grace, do you like it?" Her voice was calm and clear and sounded like that of someone older; almost like a grown-up's voice.

"Yes," I replied, "I do like it, it's about God's grace, how we can all be saved."

Biting my lip shyly, I looked down as I was still angry with God and couldn't understand why he had taken my father away and left me fatherless. Although it felt awkward talking about God, I couldn't move, I was speechless and frozen on the spot. I had never seen anyone with coffee coloured skin and green eyes before and thinking about it now, I can only describe that moment as being out of this world! Her penetrating green eyes were piercing into my soul and were affecting me in the most peculiar way. I had never seen anything like it in my life.

"I'm Amanda," she said. "What's your name?"

"Jason," I said, "but my friends call me JB."

"Whatever's going on over there?" she interrupted.

From across the street came a jeering voice, "Footballer, you ain't no footballer."

I turned to see two boys on the opposite pavement squaring up for a fight, one of them was my brother Richard.

As I was about to say, "oh I…"

"Do you know them?" she asked.

I said, "yeah, his name's Gareth and…"

"Not friends with them, are you?" she asked.

I said, "Um, well…"

"Hey JB! mummy's boy I'm talking to you!" shouted Gareth, "I'm about to pulverise your brother mate. Watch him squeal like a pig and he won't be playing much football after this, ha-ha-ha!"

As he spoke Richard flew at him and the two were locked in an ugly mess of writhing limbs, their fists pounding one another desperately. I wasn't a small eight-year-old, I was quite big for my size. One of the advantages of being big was that it made others afraid of me and it made me a little bit fearless. The disadvantage was that my brother would often tease me and demand that I would back him up when he got into a fight. The only problem was that it happened too often.

Well, on this particular day, I wasn't prepared to fight anyone. The girl with the green eyes had my full attention, I was stuck, glued in position and couldn't move. I could hear my brother shouting at me to help him, but for the first time I found myself ignoring him. I was mesmerised by Amanda, then suddenly, she sprang to her feet, whilst clutching her dolls and hairbrush in one hand, she wagged the forefinger of the other hand at my brother and Gareth, who were both locked in full combat.

"Stop it! Stop that at once do you hear! What will your parents think?"

The pair stood rooted to the pavement and gawked at her for a moment; sheer surprise reflection in their faces. Then Gareth sneered, "what? he ain't got no dad, if you must know, his dad's dead!"

Echoing him, Richard then shouted even more vehemently, "yeah, dead! dead! so will you be if you don't shut your mouth!"

"I'll call the police," retorted Amanda, without intimidation.

"Good," spat Gareth, "Cause I'm about to kill the both of you, you idiots, you and him." He swung a violent punch at Richard at the very moment when the two removal men appeared from Amanda's house, shouting at all of us. Gareth promptly ran off around the corner swearing obscenely, whilst my brother walked away very upset. The moving men, shaking their heads in disapproval, resumed unloading furniture from the van.

Amanda returned to her place on the steps, and to the slow rhythmical combing of her doll's hair. "Was that really your brother?" she asked.

"Hmm," I murmured.

"And is it true about your father, that he's dead?" Amanda asked.

"Yes," I replied.

"I'm very sorry," Amanda said.

I nodded, not knowing what to say.

Amanda asked, "why was the other one saying your brother wasn't a footballer?"

"Because he is, my brother I mean. He's a really good footballer and talent scouts come to see him play on Saturdays. Gareth is jealous and doesn't like it. For some reason my brother just seems to be a magnet for trouble and he gets into fights. Being his brother, I find myself getting into fights because of him and I hate it! He starts the fights then drags me into them and we go home bruised and battered."

Amanda responded "Oh."

I watched her combing the dolls' hair for a moment then mumbled, "well, I'd better go in for my tea now, bye then."

"Bye JB."

All the way home I thought about this peculiar girl and had a strange feeling in my stomach. I was daydreaming about her, not paying much attention to anything until I was suddenly brought back to earth by the voice of my brother swearing at me. He was mad. He had just been beaten up and much as I didn't want to care about his fighting antics, I felt sorry for him.

I looked up and saw him running towards me, he was beginning to turn his aggression towards me. I ran and ran and did all I could to prevent him from beating me up. I had never seen so much anger coming from my brother before.

That night I dreamt about my dad; that we were on a small boat together in the middle of the ocean, both of us looking out for land. In the water nearby, my brother Richard had a football and he was using it to try and keep afloat, but I could see he was starting to sink. Then I saw another boat and in it was Amanda, singing her song. When she saw us, she smiled as she sailed by. I looked back at my brother and then at Amanda and did not know which way to go.

3

◼ A Sense of Uncertainty

"Come on Jason, please, we'll be late."

It was Sunday and as usual my mum wanted me to go to church with her. I didn't really want to go but knew I had no choice. The walking to church was the bit that I disliked the most. It was only a few minutes away, but every step I took had me bracing myself, waiting for the appearance of Gareth and his boys. Sometimes, seeing the steely look in my mother's eyes as she marched me briskly along the road, would stop them from actually calling out. She had been known to get the police on them before; not that it had done any good. They would vanish long before the patrol car came crawling by. But it made them that little bit wary of her. If I had been seen on my own approaching the church it would have been no contest and I would probably be lying in the gutter bleeding, whilst hearing their mocking laughter and shouts of "mummy's boy" and "Bible basher" as they tore off on their bikes.

"Come on," she said again, seeing that I was still sitting reluctantly on the sofa. "Comb your hair and let's get going."

I said, "What about Richard?"

My replied, "Never mind him."

"He never goes," I said using my usual line of defense.

"You want to do everything your brother does?" she asked. "If he put his head in the oven would you do the same?", this was her usual response. It covered up for the fact that she had lost the power to either influence or control my brother. It seemed that no-one could really; unless it was a football scout or perhaps people like Gareth.

The journey was uneventful, and I was relieved. Going home would be fine as there was always a crowd coming out of church that I could hide amongst. In any case, Gareth and his mates would be off on their day's activities by then, vandalizing or breaking into places where they shouldn't be.

As we took our places in church, I glimpsed a familiar figure. In the pew opposite was Amanda; the girl with the green eyes, coffee coloured skin and lovely singing voice. She was sitting with a dark chocolate skinned woman.

"Don't stare at people," chided my mother whilst nudging my arm. "Oh, it's Maureen and Amanda." She gave them a smile and the lady with the dark chocolate skin nodded politely.

"Do you know them?" I asked.

My mum responded, "Uh huh."

"So, is that her mum?"

"Of course," whispered my mother.

I said, "she's a lot darker."

My mum said, "she's from Ghana, her dad is white, and anyway, don't make personal remarks about people."

"So, where is he?", I asked.

"Where's who?" My mother was studying the order of service.

"Her dad," I said.

"I don't know dear, now please pray."

Mum took off her glasses and knelt down in silence. Clasping my palms dutifully together and leaning my head against them, I turned ever so slightly and gazed across the aisle.

At school the following day I saw Amanda again. She was standing in the playground, her green eyes looking down at the doll she was holding in her hands.

"Want to play with the girls do you, mummy's boy?"

I looked around to see Gareth and two of his mates, their arms spread-eagled provocatively against the chain link fence, leering at me. They were on the other side, out on the street. Although they were all of secondary school age, they rarely seemed to attend. My brother Richard, who was at the same school had said that Gareth had been suspended a few times and could be expelled soon, meaning he wasn't allowed to go back.

As I turned to walk away one of Gareth's mates shouted, "Not surprised, mummy's boy? Even your so-called wuss of a brother is still going to school. What a wuss mate, what a wuss!" Amanda had come out of her reverie now and was staring at them. I thought, at any moment, she was going to give them a telling off as she had done that day outside her house. Instead, she just continued to stare, the doll hanging more limply than before, her face wreathed in thought, as if trying to make her mind up about something.

I looked at Amanda and she noticed me staring at her. "Can I help you?" she yelled over to me. I could hardly talk as yet again her green eyes had got me. I was like a rabbit frozen in the headlamp of an oncoming car. Wanting to start a conversation, I stuttered the few words that I could muster, "You must be eight years old like me," I said.

"Pardon me! I am ten years old and I don't normally hang around with people younger than me."

"Erm…" I stuttered "as I watched Amanda walk away. "I'm going to be ten soon," she said.

That evening when I got home, Richard let me in.

"Where's Mum?" I asked.

He shrugged, made a face at me as if I had said something dumb. Then he picked up his football from the hall, booted it into the street and ran after it.

I thought it was rather strange Mum being out, because she always made a point of being back from work by the time I got home from school. It was also funny how Richard was home so early, as his school was a bus ride away and he never normally got back before me.

Six o'clock came, then seven, and still there was no sign of Mum, or of Richard. It started to get dark, so I drew the curtains and looked in the fridge for something to eat. There were some cold sausages, so I buttered a few slices of bread and made a sandwich and had a glass of milk. I watched some TV for a bit and then went up to my bedroom. Mum must have been held up at work I thought. But why hadn't she called? I went to her bedroom and lifted the receiver on the telephone by her bed. I wanted to check the phone was working, and then thought maybe I should ring the police, but what would I say? I didn't want mum to get into trouble for leaving me at home on my own. Then again, she might have had an accident, and where was Richard?

I didn't know what to do, and at about eleven o'clock I climbed into my bed. I was awake for a long time with the light on, listening for the door downstairs but there was nothing, not a sound; it felt weird. I couldn't remember ever being alone before, was this how mum felt when dad died, I wondered? But he was gone forever, gone to Heaven, my mum was coming back; at least I hoped she was.

4

▪ Lead Us Not into Temptation

The following morning, I opened my eyes with a feeling that something wasn't right, but for those few seconds between sleep and waking I couldn't place what it was. When I remembered, I leapt out of bed and ran downstairs. On the sofa, dressed in her clothes with her eyes closed, lay my mum. Her shoes and handbag were strewn on the floor. My heart pounded as for an instant, I had a horrible fear she was dead. Then with relief I saw her shoulder move slightly as she let out a sigh and turned over. I tiptoed to the kitchen, got some breakfast and got ready for school. She was still asleep when I let myself quietly out of the house, there was still no sign of Richard.

I dawdled as I approached Amanda's house from the opposite side of the road. I was hoping to run into her as she left. I knew her mum took her to school in the car most days, but occasionally she walked. It would be a good chance to talk, as I didn't dare approach her in the playground for fear of ridicule. Gareth and his gang aside, the other kids in school thought she was strange and had an awkward demeanor about her.

As I drew level with her front door, I heard a noise coming from within. Someone, a woman, was shouting her head off about something: her tone reproachful and bitter. Then came a man's voice, the words were indistinct, but the exchange was very heated. You could almost smell the anger in the air, like a poisonous gas. Suddenly the door opened, and Amanda and her mum appeared, their faces tense as they hurried to the car. I was curious but felt I did not want them to see me staring, or to know that I had heard the argument. At that moment I felt very sorry for Amanda.

I supposed the man's voice had been Amanda's father, though I had never seen him, I was confused. From the way she spoke so eloquently, I had always thought of her family as being very proper, and to hear her parents arguing in such an ugly way was a shock.

In the playground Amanda stood alone clutching her doll, a distant dreamy look on her face. With a beating heart I walked over and said, "hi."

"The word is hello," she replied, "don't you have any manners?"

I felt hurt by her harsh, sarcastic tone, "what's wrong with him, everyone says it."

I then said, "do you want to be like everyone, that's what my mum says."

"What?" Amanda exclaimed.

"She says I shouldn't be like my brother Richard, but I can't help it sometimes; especially if he's in trouble, I have to try and defend him."

Then Amanda said, "he shouldn't get into trouble in the first place. There are ways to behave you know. Well, no, obviously you don't."

Amanda never looked at me as she spoke, instead her eyes were fixed on the sky. As if she was reaching for some higher place, a world away from where she was. A place where everyone spoke and behaved properly; somewhere where she obviously thought she belonged, rather than down here with people like me.

All of a sudden, I felt a strange mood arising in me. It was like a storm or like a flash of bright lightning that reveals something in you that you never knew was there. Something that you don't want others to see in you. I was ANGRY! Was this what the other kids saw in Amanda and said about her? That behind those enchanting green eyes, that sweet singing voice and her beautiful coffee coloured skin, Amanda was just a prissy stuck-up little cow?

As the storm continued to rage inside me, I fought back how I was feeling, trying to hold on to some calm. I pushed those mean evil thoughts away as I stood there beside her and as she continued to stare into space; looking so superior. But the feeling of rage, was winning the battle, how dare she talk to me like that? Who does she think she is? I could no longer find in my heart the sorrow and sympathy I had felt for her just a few hours ago. Her family wasn't perfect, I knew that now. Her dad never went to church and was obviously secretly fighting his own demons. As for her mum, she just dragged Amanda along to church to keep up appearances. Amanda, this pest of a girl! A stuck-up little missy telling me how I ought to behave, how dare she? And she had slagged-off my brother too, I've had it with her. She wasn't perfect but pretended she was and was just putting on an act.

She was still staring at the sky and for some reason this just made me even angrier towards her. I could feel the blood pumping in my head. I opened my mouth to say something horrible to her, but the words just wouldn't come out. I turned and walked off but felt upset with myself for not letting her have it, she needed to learn some respect.

 Richard let me in again that evening, but mum was at home, she apologised for being out late the previous night and explained that she had been a bit under the weather. There were bags under her eyes and she looked like she had been crying. There was a sad empty feeling in the pit of my stomach, and I felt as if I was going to cry myself. I wanted to sit and talk to my mum but instead I just murmured "okay," and switched on the TV.

Mum made us all some dinner and at about half past seven, said she was tired and was going to have an early night. "Turn everything off before you go to bed, there's good boys." She then kissed each of us on our foreheads, said "God bless you" and went upstairs. No sooner had she left the room than Richard sprang from the sofa, fetching his trainers and jacket from the hall he said, "right, I'm out of here, don't wait up kid."

"Where are you going?" I asked.

"To have some fun," Richard replied.

I said, "but it's nearly dark."

"That's when you have the most fun," he parted his lips in a clever, mischievous smile.

"What time will you be back?" I asked.

"Who knows?" his smile grew wider, who cares?"

I looked back at the television, a nature programme was showing a shark, prowling the depths of the ocean, and was making its way remorselessly towards a shoal of fish. The shark's mouth opened revealing gleaming teeth that filled the screen as it came closer.

"Are you coming," he said, standing by the door looking at me with a facial expression on his face, he had never used with me before, it was the look of an equal.

I stared back at the screen for a few seconds and without speaking, put on my coat and trainers, and followed my brother into the gathering darkness.

5

Thieves in the Night

That night was scary but kind of exciting at the same time, we must have walked for about half an hour; over fields and across a railway bridge, until we got to what looked like a warehouse. Richard led me around the back of the building, through stinging nettles and weeds as tall as our shoulders. He then reached into his jacket and took out a thin metal bar, which was flattened at one end. Where he had got it from, I had no idea. Sliding the flat end into the doorframe, he yanked it hard a couple of times. The wooden frame started to split with a loud creaking noise that filled the night air. My heart was beating fast and I was about to run off, but Richard grabbed my arm and said, "come on!" The door was off its hinges and we were in. Suddenly an alarm went off frightening the life out of me, I froze. Richard hissed at me, and said, "let's do this and get out of here."

He seemed to know where he was going, and flashing a torch went straight over to some packages stacked up against a wall. They were boxes of cigarettes, hundreds of them piled right up to the ceiling. "Fill this, now," he said and shoved a black bin liner in my hand and frantically I scooped the packages into the bag, while he did the same with another. The alarm was still going like crazy and I was feeling sick with panic. A few seconds later, I was running back through the nettles, down the track and over the railway bridge. Richard was just in front of me, and I could hear him laughing, a mad hysterical laugh of triumph and relief.

On the following Saturday Richard gave me some money from the cigarettes he'd sold. Over the next few weeks he took me out again, breaking into houses, stores and one night the back of a pub, where this massive dog came after us. I thought I was going to die. We had stolen some bottles of whiskey and dropping one as we legged it over a fence, it crashed on the concrete. Lights started coming on and I heard people shouting. How we made it home that night I don't know. That was the night I first realized there was something seriously wrong with my mum. I don't mean physically, although she did look kind of ill, but it was her mood that was all wrong. She had been out a lot herself lately, and one-time Richard and I had seen her stumbling up the path as we were returning from one of our expeditions. I can remember waiting at the corner of the road until she had gone inside but watching my mum struggling to unlock the door made me feel uneasy. I must talk to her, I kept telling myself. As both Richard and I entered the house I could see a feint shadow on the sofa. The house was in darkness and silence filled the living room as we both crept in unsure of who was there. I almost jumped out of my skin when I heard my mother's voice. Suddenly she arose and switching the lights on, asked "And where have you two been?" With the whiskey bottles in our hand, mum looked at the two of us. If she hadn't already guessed what Richard and I were up to, she had found out for sure. She had been curled up on the sofa, almost buried under the cushions. The weird thing was she didn't sound angry, it was as if she didn't care anymore, as if she had given up on us. Giving up on Richard I could understand but I was only a kid, she stood up and grabbed Richard's bag. Looking inside, again she seemed neither surprised nor cross. She just pulled out the whiskey and said, "thanks Rich, I could do with a drink." Tucking the bottle under her arm, mum shuffled off into the kitchen.

Richard shrugged his shoulders and disappeared up to bed. I sat in the living room wondering if mum was going to talk to me and what I would say if she did. But the only sound from the kitchen was the occasional chink of a glass. I sat for a long time with the realisation that mum hadn't only given up on us, but she had also given up on herself.

The next day I sat in school in a daze, I realized how tired I was from the late nights, and the adrenalin that I'd become hooked on when going out stealing with Richard. But it wasn't a good feeling anymore and being honest, it never had been. I was sick of it now and knew it wasn't right. I had let my brother lead me astray and all because I wanted to gain his respect.

A few months had passed and during one break-time at school I looked across the playground and saw Amanda. I had not spoken to her since the day she had been rude to me. It was literally a few months, but it felt like years. I guess I had wanted to prove a point to her by staying away but looking back now, Amanda had become quite a popular girl in school and didn't miss me as much as I was expecting her to. She probably didn't even care what I did or thought. I wasn't part of her world anymore and she had made loads of friends. If the truth be known I felt awful. I did miss her and knew I had a crush on her and wanted her to like me too. I knew deep down that I had always wanted that, and that's why I had been so upset when she talked down to me.

My Dick Turpin adventures with my brother Richard added no value to my life and they had left me feeling bad. On top of that, I was now invisible to Amanda and my mum, who was about to give up on life. What have I got to be happy about? My life was becoming more and more miserable each day. My stomach churned as I thought about these things. What had happened to me? I thought of my dad and how sad he would be to see his family like this. It felt like I was heading towards the edge of a cliff and the only person who could pull me back was me, it wasn't too late. I felt totally alone but I had to do something because there was no-one else.

I looked across at Amanda again, who seemed to be lost in her own little world. She was totally oblivious of everything and I remember saying to myself, *being horrible to me was the worst thing you could have ever done.* Why I said that, I don't know but I later concluded that Amanda was like a beacon; a lighthouse in the darkness of night and where my troubled soul would soon find peace again. But not having that beacon, made my life a dark and lonely place.

6

▪ Paying The Price

Two and a half years had passed after the death of my dad and I was now almost ten years old. During those troublesome years, I watched my brother's life deteriorate and lived with the pain of seeing my mum, whom I loved, become unrecognisable. It was obvious that my father's death had caused this. I could no longer blame God and I had come to terms with the fact that things happen that we have no control over, I called it "Life."

During those times when mum stayed out till very late, the amount of alcohol she drank was, in my opinion, excessive. And ninety per cent of the time my mum came home drunk. Richard was hardly at home and by this time I was very comfortable with looking after myself, I had become a microwave chef and a food label genius. However, one day something inside me said 'enough is enough,'. I remember falling to the floor and screaming out, "I want my mum! I want to be normal again!" Church was the one thing that made mum happy and perhaps going back might make her happy again. *I know!* I said to myself. *I will suggest it to her and I will go with her for support."*

I was nervous about suggesting that we should go back to church. After all, it had been about a year and a half since the last time she had gone—and she was always the one dragging me along. But now It was my turn to do the persuading. How funny was that? The hardest bit was plucking up the courage to open my mouth and say the words. "Let's go to church on Sunday mum." For a good half minute, she stared at me in silence. It was as if her mind was struggling to adjust to this change in our relationship, just like I was. She was the mother, I was the child and she was supposed to take care of me; give me advice, instructions and all the rest of it but this was the other way around. I hoped it didn't sound too wrong that she wouldn't feel awkward and embarrassed at the fact that I had seen she needed help.

"Well this is a surprise," she said, "I'm glad you're showing some interest in doing the right thing for once."

I had to let that go, after all, she was my mum. "Of course, Jason, I will go with you on Sunday." Well I wasn't expecting that and yes, I couldn't stop smiling, I've got my mum back.

When we got to church that Sunday, Amanda was there with her mother, she glanced over at me at one point and when our eyes met, turned quickly away. We hadn't spoken properly, just a quick hello and bye every time we met, but me being me, I had no control over how I really felt about her. I was smitten and not ashamed to say it, at the moment she looked at me my heart swelled. Everything was going to be alright and I suddenly felt uplifted as if I was getting my life back again, unfortunately, it wasn't going to be so simple.

The next day after school, I met Amanda outside her house and tried to talk to her, expecting that after the way she had looked at me in church, she would want to be friends again. Not that she was unfriendly when I spoke to her on this occasion, but she seemed distant and I found that I was making all the effort. At first, I felt despondent but then thought, *"No, this is a challenge and I'm going to take it on. I know she likes me really and I'm not going to give up on her."* I had got my mum going to church again, that had taken the courage, and it worked, and so it would be with Amanda. I thought to myself, *"she may not want to talk to me today but there is always tomorrow."*

But Mum's problems were not so easily cured. Church was good, it was her place, but she just wasn't the same person I had always known her to be. I spoke to one of the church leaders about it, which again took some doing. Mum was quite a reserved, personal lady that kept things close as she would say, but I thought why not as I wanted to see mum happy again. The church leader handed me a leaflet that had the details of a counsellor on it. As soon as I got home, I passed the number to my mum and told her what the church leader said. Just like when I had suggested going back to church, she stared into space for a while then nodded and said she would do it. She went on to say that I was a good son for thinking of her like that; I could see she was welling up. All at once I felt both proud and humbled at the same time and sorry for my mum. I was fighting back the tears but felt like I needed to have a good old cry. It was a little bit embarrassing for me, but it felt awesome at the same time. Like the beginning of an unnerving but special new time for us all. If only Richard was around too, he hadn't been seen for days.

I wasn't the only one wondering where he was, that evening there was a knock at the door. It was two police officers who were looking for Richard. Mum's face was rigid with worry said, "can I help you officers?" They said nothing but turned to me instead, my pulse was racing, and my mouth felt as dry as sandpaper. "And you must be Jason," said the senior officer.

"What do you want with him?" demanded my mum, "and what's my Richard supposed to have done anyway?"

One of the police officers replied calmly, "did we say he'd done anything?" Do you smoke Jason, or like the taste of whiskey?"

My mum was getting agitated now, "I want a solicitor, you've no right talking to him without a solicitor, you have no right to be in my house."

One police man said, "very well then madam, I think it's best if we all go down to the station and sort this out, you too, we've a car waiting outside when you're ready."

The police station was scary, with no pleasurable thrill whatsoever attached. My mum seemed as steady as a rock when we got there and assured me that she wasn't going to let them do anything to me or take me anywhere without her. In a way, me being in trouble seemed to have snapped her out of her depression and brought her to her senses. She was more like her old strong self again. The police officer said that both Richard and I had been identified on a CCTV camera, breaking into licensed premises a few years back and that one of the suspects was seen entering the premises again a few days ago. But this time, the owner wanted to press charges, I began to cry as confusion and anxiety crept in. Could I go to prison for something that I had done years ago?

A loud sobbing broke out when this latest shocking thing hit my poor mother, her tears fell. She had not seen Richard for what felt like weeks and now I was at the police station with her, fearing that I will spend the rest of my days rotting away in a prison cell with nothing but bread to eat and water to drink.

7

■ Boyhood to Manhood

When certain things happen in your life, a saying sometimes springs to mind. Often such sayings will provide comfort, but other times you're reminded that though the Lord is merciful, such mercy is to temper justice, and that if we disobey his teachings, that justice can be applied sternly. One phrase that rang in my head from the day I was taken to the police station was, "let him that stealeth, steal no more."

I had followed my brother into temptation and stolen. Not so much for gain, but to impress and please him. Perhaps those sins, the sins of vanity, were worse than greed. Now I was paying in fear and apprehension of what lay ahead. My mother kept assuring me that as a first-time offender and because of my age, I would be let off lightly. But how could anyone be sure? The police asked me repeatedly where my brother was. But he had disappeared and neither me, nor, to her utter distress, did my mum know of his whereabouts. I wondered if the police thought I was lying. I also wrestled with what I would do if I did know where Richard was. Would I turn him in out of fear?

As the police officer processed my paper work, I was charged with burglary and told that I would be sent a date to appear in court. My mum was not too pleased and all I kept asking myself was would this put her back into a state of depression and would my life on this downward spiral.

"You're free to go now Mrs Bryan but please keep your son in check," said the officer as my mum looked at me, her teeth clenched, and frustration etched in the lines around her eyes… "And remember we are still looking for your other son, Richard"

The question of how my mother was feeling, and what would happen when I got to court, haunted me as the date drew near.

A week before the dreaded day, my mum received a call from the police. I was trying to be brave as I eavesdropped on her conversation. Then suddenly there was this loud shout of "Hallelujah!" The phone dropped then my mum ran towards me and kissed me all over my face.

"Mum the phone. You've dropped the phone." I could hardly pronounce the words because of the kissing but she soon got the message, ran back to the phone and made her apologies. Then she hung up.

"Jason, you're free to go. The pub owner has dropped the charges. They were really after Richard and not you but because they can't find Richard the owner has decided it wasn't worth pursuing."

With tears in her eyes mum said, "Jason, I hope you have learned your lesson. We have been asked to visit the police station next week; one of the officers wants to have a chat with you." Out of the corner of my eye I was aware of her every move but tried not to look in her direction lest we both start to cry. At the same time, I was shrewd enough to realise that I must also look repentant, which I certainly was.

When we got to the police station, a burly officer who seemed to be at least ten-feet tall sat me on a chair and began to lecture me about the consequences of being on the wrong side of the law.

Listening to him speak about what I had done, it all felt unreal, as if they were talking about someone else. I wanted to blurt out, "I'm not a bad person. I go to church, I try hard at school, I love my mum, and a hundred-and-one other things. But I just carried on listening whilst being stared at by passing police officers. The talking must have only lasted five minutes, but it felt like an eternity. I could feel myself swaying as I tried to stop myself shaking. Then I heard this woman, who looked as though she was in charge say to me, "Go home and behave yourself. If ever there is a next time, you will be facing serious trouble." I couldn't believe it. I was a changed person but felt like a criminal who was being reprimanded. Looking across the room, I knew my mum was crying and this time it was tears of relief. That night I remembered to pray to the Lord, thanking him for giving me a second chance. I prayed for Richard too and asked that he might come to no harm, and be returned to us safely, and even for his dream of becoming a professional footballer to come true. I felt uncomfortable about including that request in my prayers. I felt as though I was asking for too much. But it wasn't for myself that I was asking. I feared for Richard now and felt that if only his wish could be fulfilled it would transform him; make him the good person that I knew he was underneath. All my mum and I truly wanted though, was for him to come home and be with us as a family again.

There had been one other request on my prayer list that night, and that was for Amanda to love and respect me. But not just that, I also wanted her to somehow be mine. I wasn't old enough to understand love, but I knew what I wanted. When I first met her, I had pictured myself getting married to her, holding her close and living happily ever after and the thought of it had never left me. It felt like God's grace had given me a fresh start and by the Lord's grace, I was free from the worry of going to prison. Dare I expect to be granted this other, ultimate gift of being loved by the most beautiful girl in the world? The girl with the coffee-coloured skin and green eyes, whom I had so long adored?

My life resumed to a sort of calm but at times it felt like a slightly weird dream. At home my mum continued to struggle. She had taken advice and was now receiving counselling and psychiatric help. Word of this had somehow got around at school, where the worst elements who seized on any opportunity to exploit other peoples' troubles, made cruel remarks about my mother being "a nutter" or "being mental" or a "looney." Some though, showed kindness and I was surprised when people who I might least have expected to, came up to me and asked genuinely how my mum was doing, and wished her well again.

My brother Richard remained at large. Still apparently on the police wanted list for other crimes he had committed. He occasionally returned home, causing my mother great joy and distress in almost equal measure. Begging him to come home, she would interrogate him; where was he living, was he eating, was he well, how did he support himself etc. In fact, he looked healthy and well adjusted, but gave away little about his circumstances. On his brief visits home, he would first look me over with a slightly wary eye, then engage me in terse conversation—his residual sneer at my "goody two shoes" existence and fondness for attending church. Try as he might, he was unable to quite conceal his emotional need to maintain a connection with both Mum and me. This fact gave me a sense of relief. Rich, like all of us, was human and vulnerable and craved at whatever level, something we might loosely call love. The word love should not of course be used loosely, but it can mean so many different things. It was not at that time something to be talked about among my peers at school, certainly not at the age we had suddenly become. I had learned about puberty and the facts of life in health and social studies, and through the often lewd and coarse remarks of older and even, worryingly, younger boys.

But when the changes I had heard so much about began to take place in my own mind and body, all the prior theoretical knowledge seemed inadequate for the experience itself. It was both exciting and alarming. In any one day, I would go through a see-sawing range of emotions. Pride in my newfound sense of "manliness" was often accompanied by a hidden anxiety about the physical manifestations, especially in the company of my peers; both boys and girls. The intense, pulsing thrills of sexual attraction carried with them an equally intense frustration, and an unspoken current of shame and embarrassment, despite what all the textbooks and leaflets on "what to expect in adolescence" assured their young readers was "natural." When my fellow pupils boasted of their exploits, real or invented, with girls, I would join in with their knowing laughter, giving the lie that I too was well experienced in such matters.

Privately though I was proud of my chastity and the purity of my heart. It was like I was a spy or double agent, presenting a tough worldly cynical, "grown-up" face to my so-called mates, while the real me stood apart, waiting for my one true love. I watched Amanda, from a distance, and felt that she too was watching me as she underwent her own changes. She had gone from the sweet yet strangely confident little girl I had first set eyes upon, sitting on the front steps of her new house, to something more beautiful and even mysterious to me. A day that now seemed so long ago. She was becoming a young woman. There was talk about her parents' continued difficulties, and my Mum, blissfully unaware of the fire that burned in my heart for Amanda, would sometimes tell me what she had seen and heard, the raised voices, the coming and going of the father, the crying of the mother. Amanda must have cried too I thought. In my dreams, waking and sleeping, I pictured the time when I would come to her, hold her tightly in my arms and wipe her tears away. Never for a second did I doubt that this moment would one day arrive.

8

▪ First Kiss

Amanda and I were now attending the same school though she were two school years ahead of me. I had always dreamed of the day when we would have our first kiss, but somehow knew it might not ever happen because she saw me as this little boy who was her junior. In my mind, now that I had passed through the stages of adolescence, surely age had no bearing.

In fact, that moment came sooner than I imagined. It was towards the end of the spring term and I was on my way home from school. Passing Amanda's house, I slowed my pace as usual, looking back and forth along the road, hoping to catch a glimpse of her, or even get the chance to talk to her. I knew from the discreet looks she gave me at times, that her feelings towards me were mutual, or was I imagining it?

There was a shyness about Amanda and I soon realized this was due to an anxiety about what was happening at home and although she was a strong-minded person, there was certainly a reluctance to lay herself open emotionally. Surely, she could push past these feelings and fancy the mummy's boy that I was still known as.

Now we were both that little bit older and had passed the most crucial stage of development with the awkwardness of adolescence, conducting any kind friendship or romance was an agonising business. We had grown shy of one another, but one day I noticed a brief, longing expression that was enough for me to feed on. I convinced myself that her reluctance to talk was not "standoffish" but had a higher motive; she did not want to crack the precious mould of our love, which had grown in the hothouse silence of exchanged glances, or was I imagining this too?

"Love" was not a word I would have dared to utter to myself, let alone to Amanda. Yet, I thought if we were to actually catch each other alone one day on the way home from school, would either of us have the courage, or even desire to speak? But that day I did see her, or to be more accurate I heard her first. I had never known Amanda to cry, and so at first did not realise who was making the sobbing noise. I knew she had no siblings and it didn't sound like an adult, so I thought the crying must be from the adjacent house. Drawing close I hesitated, listening hard to the spurting, heart-rending sobbing. Then I noticed that the front door of Amanda's house was ajar. I went up the steps and pushed gently on the door, there, on the hall floor, sat Amanda, her shoulders heaving, her head in her hands.

"Amanda," I said softly, the shoulders stopped moving then slowly she raised her head. The coffee coloured skin was smirched with wet tears, the green eyes blurred as they tried to focus and I said, "what's the matter?"

Amanda said, "my dad's gone, left us I mean, gone for good."

I said, "oh, I'm really sorry."

"It doesn't matter," she blurted. Her nose was blocked from crying and she sounded as if she had a cold and continued, "nothing matters anymore." She sounded angry now and hung her head again. "Your dad died didn't he, and you got over it, so I'm sure I'll get over my dad walking out, better off without him really."

"I didn't really get over it," I replied, then immediately realized this was the wrong thing to say. I realized I should talk about her sadness, not mine, "I'm sorry."

"No, no," said Amanda shaking her head irritably, "I shouldn't have mentioned your dad, that's not fair, I just have to accept this."

"Why is your door open?" I asked, I was feeling awkward now and couldn't think of anything else to say but nobody kept doors open in our street, it was asking for trouble. Gareth and his boys were now terrorising the neighbourhood. Then I suddenly realized, she wanted someone to hear, but not just someone. She had hoped it would be me; that I would come to her, I asked, "is your mum in?"

Amanda shook her head, "she's had to go and sort some things out, she'll be back in about an hour, do you want to come in?" She got up and led me into her house, I had never been in there before, though I had imagined doing so many times. It was much like my own home; a modern three-piece suite, TV, carpets, all nicely kept. As we sat down next to each other on the sofa I felt suddenly really tongue-tied and nervous, as if I was doing something I shouldn't be doing. The next minute my heart was racing with excitement as I felt Amanda's head loll onto my shoulder. I could feel the warmth of her soft young body pressed against mine and smell the sweet fragrances of her perfume and her breath. I wondered, are we going to kiss? We did, and it was like a dream come true, an electrifying sensation as our lips met. Then the soft moist insides of our mouths, I felt like I was going to faint. Could this really be happening—was I really kissing Amanda?

I don't know how long we kissed for, but it stopped suddenly when a voice called out, "Amanda! Why in goodness name have you left the front door open?" Amanda's mum strode into the room. Though we had leapt apart immediately when we had heard her, it must have been fairly obvious what had been happening as the expressions on our faces were enough. Amanda's mum looked at me for a second, then said breezily, "Oh hello Jason, how are you, would you like a cup of tea?" She looked and sounded quite business-like, as if everything was under control, but I guessed that was just her way of dealing with the situation. "Amanda why haven't you offered Jason a cup of tea?"

"Oh, that's all right, "I said, "I've got to go home now anyway." I got up and Amanda followed me to the door.

"Text me?" she said.

"Ok, oh, what's your number?"

Amanda gave me her number, then seeing some of her classmates coming along the road, shut the door quickly without saying another word.

9

▪ Walking On Air

A A strange and magical thing had happened. I had heard people on TV and in films and books talk about being in love, but it had never had any real meaning for me. Among most of my so-called friends it was something to laugh at. Girls were not there to be "loved", that was for mummy's boys. No, girls were there to get pleasure from, to compete with, to get the better of. Love had always seemed like a no-no; a weird, sickly, weak way of living that would only give you grief if you chased it or even half-believed in it. Where girls were concerned, falling in love was falling for a trick, one that would only end up hurting you. That's what my brother Richard had always tried to teach me. There was a part of me that listened to him but never truly believed him. I kept wondering about this magical thing called love, and that kept hoping that it might exist for me. If love really existed, then there was only one place, one person in whom I would find this perfect happiness. And now I know it to be true.

I have found this hidden treasure in a girl named Amanda. Just saying her name under my breath sent my heart racing, pulsing with the memory of her soft kisses, her head leaning on my shoulder, the promise in her enchanting green eyes.

The spring had turned the trees green, the parks and gardens along the streets had color and my heart and soul were brimming with emotion and desire. I felt I wanted to be kind to everyone. I felt that I had suddenly found my place in the world and each time I exchanged a look with Amanda, across the playground, I was more pleased with my life than ever before. Our meetings were still only brief; aware of prying eyes and wagging tongues. We knew instinctively that neither of us wanted to display our love or set ourselves up for ridicule. We took our chances where we could and passing each other in the corridor Amanda might whisper quickly, "come, round after school tonight." This way we saw each other perhaps two or three times a week. It was all very innocent, tea and TV, with some kisses when her mum was busy in the kitchen. I could imagine how my brother Richard would react if I ever dared tell him about this. His sneers and provocations at such old-fashioned un-cool behavior with a girl, at my lamentable lack of 'progress', to me it was the opposite. Whilst my desires were burning away, and I wanted with every fibre of my body to 'go further' with Amanda. At the same time there was ecstasy in not doing so, an ecstasy I knew she shared as we sat close on the sofa; feeling the warmth of each other's bodies through our clothes, catching our breath between the stolen kisses.

I had not yet asked Amanda to my house; one reason was the worry that Richard might pay us one of his unexpected visits, at a moment when we were there together. And much as I was always pleased to see my brother, I did not want his world to collide with mine and Amanda's. The day would come when they met, I felt sure, but things would be different by then. I had a perfect imaginary picture of Richard as a reformed person, still high spirited, bold and cheeky, but all for good. Perhaps a successful footballer, or a businessman with a smart car and a big house. A cool older brother, the best man at my wedding to Amanda, one big happy family, with my mum very happy and proud of us all.

Mum was doing okay, still going to her counselling and seeming to be making progress. She would sometimes have a glass of wine in the evening, but there were no more late nights out and sleeping on the sofa. She had also got herself a new job in an office and was taking pride in her appearance again. Occasionally she would shed a tear for my dad and had anxieties about Richard's bad-boy lifestyle. She had no real peace and was forever hoping that he would come home for good. Either that or that he was settled somewhere, steering clear of trouble. The one good thing about Richard being away from our neighbourhood was that he wasn't, as far as I knew, hanging around with Gareth. From talk that I had heard at school recently, it seems he had gone from bad to worse, someone said that Gareth had been locked up.

After church on Sundays my mum would often wait and talk to Amanda's mum, ask how she was doing and if she needed any help. My mum was caring that way and although her concern was genuine, I also sensed it did her good to reach out to other people. While these hushed conversations between our mothers took place in the doorway of the church, Amanda and I would exchange shy glances, acting as if we were hardly acquainted. Human beings are strange, especially in teen years, and even more so when they really like one another!

The term was coming to an end, and the long summer holidays would soon begin. Never had I looked forward to them as much. Six whole weeks off school and Amanda at home too. I pictured all the things we might do. Trips to the cinema, train rides out into the country, maybe even out to the coast; Margate or Sheerness, where my mum and dad used to take Richard and I sometimes. I felt sure my mum would be all right about it, as would Amanda's mum. We were both secondary students and old enough now to go out and about on our own. Wherever we went, whatever we did, just being with her and her alone, would be paradise. My life had been transformed and everything was suddenly so good. The real stuff, the happiness that people talked about in books, was at last beginning for me. And not just for me it seemed, but for my mother who was looking stronger and more content than she had in a long time. She had seen my brother Richard a few times, and apparently, he had a job and a flat of his own now, which had done a lot to put her mind at rest.

When the last day of term arrived, I could not wait to get home, tear off my school uniform and start making plans about seeing Amanda. I kept marvelling at the fact that we could now spend whole days together without any cares or worries in the world; it was going to be just amazing! When I walked indoors my mum also seemed excited. "Jason," she announced giving me a big smile, "I've got a surprise for you." WOW, I thought, life just keeps on getting better. I wondered what her surprise was. Dare I hope it was the new mobile phone I had been wanting for so long?

"I've taken the next three weeks off work," my mum continued, "and booked a holiday in Spain." Without thinking I replied, "great mum, you deserve it, and don't worry, I'll make sure to look after the house okay." Her grin broadened still more, "don't be silly," she laughed, "you are coming too! Now think about what you want to pack, our flight leaves tomorrow morning."

10

■ Absence Makes the Heart Grow Fonder

I felt like the ground had been swept away from beneath my feet. There I was, quietly dreaming of long walks on pebble beaches with my beloved Amanda, huddling down in some secluded spot, of bliss-filled afternoons in the darkness of the cinema with Amanda! But instead, I was to be whisked off onto a plane and forced to spend the next few weeks hundreds of miles away. I would not get to see her for ages and ages now. When you're young it can seem like forever. I wanted to run from the house. I just wanted to shout "No! No! No!" at my mother. "It's my life and I don't want to do this right now. It doesn't fit in with my plans, okay!"

But I didn't; instead I kept a big, fake stupid smile on my face, I just had to play along. She had been through a lot and knew there were times when she had not been easy to be around. Perhaps she felt as if she had let me down, I realized instantly that this was her way of saying sorry, of saying she loved me. How could I possibly tell her that I would prefer to stay home because I would rather be with a girl during the holidays? It couldn't be done, if I displayed even a trace of disappointment now, I knew it would break my mother's heart.

I let my mum pack my suitcase for me, as I could see she wanted to do it anyway. I kept thanking her, desperate to hide my real feelings. "Anyone would think it's a Porsche I'm giving you instead of a holiday in Spain. But I'm glad you appreciate it son," she chuckled as she folded my shirts neatly and laid them in the case.

"A fortnight?" I said.

"Yes, I'm sorry it can't be longer," she responded absentmindedly. I was thinking fast, okay, two weeks is better than three, two weeks is only fourteen days, and that leaves me the rest of the school holidays to see Amanda. Not so bad. Not so bad after all.

"I took three weeks leave from work, but I'm aiming to use the third week to do all the jobs that need doing around the house and in the garden."

"Oh! Two weeks. No that's brilliant," I said, "I thought you only meant a week anyway, so two weeks is doubly better."

"Doubly better, is that quite grammatical Jason?" Mum had a thing about good grammar and often called me out on my speech.

"I dunno."

"Dunno's definitely not!" She laughed and threw a beach towel at me playfully. It was good to see her laughing. And now it was like I had lost £9, only to suddenly find £3, I began to brighten up. Mum was happy, and deep down inside of me I knew that I would have a good time in Spain. Of course, I would think about Amanda every waking moment and dream about her too. But where she was concerned, there was even pleasure in that.

As it turned out, I didn't think about Amanda all the time we were in Spain. I had sent her a message the night before the flight, apologising for the short notice but it was my mum's surprise and I wanted to please mum by going. She had replied straight away, saying have a good time and looking forward to seeing me when I got back. What more could I ask for? I felt perfectly reassured, and meanwhile there were things to do that took up my time and my interest. Playing football with other boys I met on the beach; having a laugh, swimming in the hotel pool or the sea, and watching the sun go down in the evening over a burger and a coke.

My mum gave me my freedom to hang out, as long as I let her know where I was going and didn't leave the part of the beach that belonged to the hotel, she was okay about leaving me to enjoy myself. "It's your holiday too Jason, don't forget," she would say. "I know you don't want me breathing down your neck all the time like some helicopter parent!" She soon got chatting to a group of women about her own age who had come away together—it was like she had known them all her life. I was pleased for my mum and felt kind of proud of her too; seeing her confident like that with other people and the fact that they had obviously taken such a liking to her.

Even though I was having fun on holiday, Amanda was always there at the back of my mind. At various times, I would imagine her sitting with me by the pool, the two of us sharing a meal the way adults do, being real grown-up type lovers, not just a teenage boyfriend and girlfriend. Not kids but adults, if that makes sense.

In the evenings, there was a live band playing music at the outdoor restaurant. Soon enough, the music inspired people to get up to dance. Every time a couple got up to dance, I would picture Amanda and myself taking the floor with the other couples dancing, while holding her closely to me, staring into her beautiful green eyes.

One night one of the guests asked my mum to dance. I watched my mum blush. I couldn't believe she was smiling. It was strange seeing her in that situation and although it was a long time ago, I could remember her dancing like that with my dad. That was the last time she had danced probably, certainly with a man, was the slight knot in my stomach jealousy? The band was only playing upbeat disco numbers so everyone was partying; not slow stuff where you touch each other but the thought hit me like a thunderbolt. How would I feel if my mum met someone and went out with them? Suppose she got married again? It was not something I wanted to think about, so I turned my eyes away and thought instead of Amanda, and what we were going to do when I got home, it was only four days away now. *Not that I had been counting!*

11

◾ A Surprise in Store

The flight home seemed to take forever and with each passing minute, I became more and more anxious. My mum had prepared some snacks for the journey and all I kept doing was snacking. Mum looked at me, sensing my anxiety, but never said a word. To deflect the attention off me I switched on the in-flight entertainment and watched a movie. By the time I watched the first movie and was about to get on to the next movie, we stated to make our descent into Gatwick. Everything ran smoothly and quickly in passport control and customs, and our luggage was there on the carousel. Mum rang the valet parking service and by the time we reached the slip road, her car was there. "I can see you've had a good time!" she observed. She glanced at my relaxed yet eager to be home expression as she turned the key in the ignition. "Hmm, great, thanks for the holiday mum, it was the best." I could almost feel her happiness. "You're the best," she murmured fondly. I said, "I'm so happy, to have you as my mum, I love you mum." At that point I could hear my mum sniffling, my gesture of love had made her cry.

As we sped off down the motorway, heading for home, I closed my eyes and thought of Amanda, what a miracle it was that we had found each other at last. In the morning, just a few short hours from now, I would be calling at her house, and we would be in each other's arms.

It was very late when we arrived home, mum kissed me goodnight and announced she was going straight to bed; we would sort the cases out in the morning. I felt full of energy and wide-awake now. I sent Amanda a quick text just to let her know I was back safely. I wasn't expecting a reply as it was past midnight, and I knew her mum didn't like her staying up late using her computer or her phone. I laid down on my bed fully clothed and stared at the ceiling, just smiling to myself. How many of the boys I had met in Spain had a girl like Amanda to come home to? None! I knew because there was no one in the whole wide world like her.

Next morning at about ten o'clock I stood outside Amanda's house looking up at her bedroom window. The curtains were still closed, there had been no reply to my text of the previous night, but perhaps the curtains explained it, she was sleeping in. I guessed she hadn't expected me to call round so early today. I wondered if I should come back later or send her another text first. She might not like me seeing her before she had time to wash and put on make-up and stuff. Girls can be vain that way, particularly when it came to their appearance. But hey, what was I thinking? This was not just any girl, this was my Amanda, with her coffee-coloured skin and green eyes. She was naturally beautiful at any time of the day or night. She needed no make-up or smart clothes to be who she was. She was perfect! Even so, I was nervous now about barging in. I couldn't bear it if she were to find my sudden presence uncomfortable or annoying in any way.

Just as I was about to turn and leave the front door opened. "Jason?" It was Amanda's mum, a towel wrapped around her head. "Amanda's not here, she's gone to see her friend, so she says."

I nodded, "when will she be back?"

"Soon I hope, she's got to tidy her room, I shut the curtains because I don't want the good Lord looking in on her mess. It's the last time I put your things away, I told her. You gotta do it for yourself now. I don't know what's wrong with that girl Jason, truly I don't. Ever since the summer holidays started, she's been lazy and staying out of the house all hours; I don't know where. You've been on holiday, haven't you?"

"Yes, yes, with my mum."

"That's right, yes Amanda told me, how is your mum?"

I said, "very good thanks, we had a good time."

"Oh well give her my regards and tell her I'll see her in church next Sunday."

"Will Amanda be there?" I asked.

"I doubt it dear, oh heavens! I can't say anything about that girl now; I just don't understand her. She doesn't want to do anything I tell her too, she forgets she's got school work to do over the holidays – she forgets everything to be honest! Oh well, never mind. I've got to go Jason dear, I've got things to sort out. You know how it is but be sure and say hello to your mum now."

"Sure." I said.

When the door closed, I stood staring at it in bewilderment for a moment. Why wasn't Amanda at home waiting for me? I checked my phone again but there were no missed calls or messages. Then I scrolled back to my original text to her the night before going on holiday and saw that I had put today's date as the day I would get back. Phew what a relief, realizing she wouldn't be expecting me to get home until the afternoon at least. But what about the text I had sent her last night? Obviously, she hadn't seen it, her phone must be out of credit or charge or something, or maybe she had mislaid it. Her mum did say she was forgetful now. *I know, I'll come back in the afternoon,* I said to myself.

I wandered home, where my mum was unpacking our suitcases and getting the washing machine on. I felt at loose ends now and paced up and down the garden, checking the time every few minutes. At about 11.00 am my mum brought me lunch, a few sandwiches and a drink. "Don't know what to do with yourself now there's no beach eh? Didn't you have a school project to complete?" I nodded. I had been given an assignment but there was no way I could even look at that right now. "Don't you have friends to see? How about popping around to see how Amanda is, she's a nice girl."

Hearing my mum utter her name made me jump for some reason, it was so unexpected. Did my mother know more than she let on? Had I given something away somehow? I was reluctant to admit where I had been first thing. Then I remembered Amanda's mum had spoken to me. "I went past there this morning," I said casually "and saw her mum and she said to say hello." My mother nodded. "I'll look in on her, she's not having it easy with her husband gone away."

By about 1 o'clock I couldn't hold out any longer, I had sent Amanda another text and still had no reply. "I'm just going out mum," I shouted out as I slammed the door behind me. "Thought I might look in on Amanda like you said."

"That's a good idea and ask her mum for me if she would she like to come around for coffee tomorrow, she can give me a ring, she's got the number."

"OK, bye," I said

"Bye love," my mum replied.

Two minutes later I was nearing Amanda's house, as I approached, I saw the door open and her mother come out. Feeling awkward I waited out of sight until she had got in her car and drove off. I was about to cross the road when I noticed Amanda's bedroom curtains move slightly. Then from a car parked opposite someone got out, and after taking a quick look around walked up to the house inserted a key in the door and went in. I felt my whole body go faint, the person who had just entered Amanda's house was my brother Richard.

12

■ Questions

I must have stood there for a good five minutes, not moving, barely breathing, just staring up at the window. There was no further movement and the whole street seemed strangely quiet. It was as though time stood still. No birds flew by, no crickets chirped, no dogs barked in the distance—everything had frozen in place. When I eventually tore my eyes away and began to retrace my steps, I could feel myself shaking. My mind, which had until now been numb with shock, was working furiously. I was trying to think of a reason, any innocent reason, why Richard would not only be calling at Amanda's house, but letting himself in with a key. He also appeared to be driving, when to the best of my knowledge he didn't even have a license. Was he even old enough for one? Though I hadn't set eyes on him in months, it seemed impossible that he could have suddenly passed his driving test. And as for the car, although it hadn't looked new, I suspected there was no way he could have acquired it honestly.

But was I being too harsh? Richard had been dishonest in the past, but so had I and if I could turn over a new leaf, why couldn't he? Maybe he had borrowed the car. I remembered hearing him talking about starting a car cleaning business, collecting and returning the vehicles would be part of the service. But that didn't explain the key to Amanda's house. Amanda—oh God no! The thought of what might be going on in there right now, made me feel sick! I had to find out. I had to know for sure what was going on, so I turned and walked as boldly as I could back to the house.

The door opened within a couple of minutes of my knocking. Amanda stood there, dressed in jeans and a T-shirt, her hair tied back, her coffee-coloured skin as beautiful as ever. Her green eyes widened when she saw me.

"Jason!" she said.

"Hi," I said, trying desperately to keep my voice steady, as if everything was normal.

"Did you have a nice holiday?", she asked.

"Hmm, yeah, thanks, did you get my text?" I replied.

"Text? Oh no, no, my phone got nicked," she said.

I had never heard her say "nicked" before and why wasn't she asking me in? As if reading my thoughts, she opened the door wider. "Come in, you'll never guess who's here," she said.

"Who?" I was shaking again.

"Your big brother!" She seemed different somehow, her voice, her manner, I couldn't put my finger on it but there was something different about her. Richard sat in the kitchen, he extended his fist to mine with a low growl, "Bro! I hear you been to Spain."

"Oh, yeah, with mum, she wanted to take you too, but we didn't know where you were" I tailed off guiltily, as if I was somehow in the wrong.

Richard responded, "Been busy man, busy."

I asked, "what are you doing here?" It was a strain to make it sound friendly.

Richard said, "grafting," he grinned and pointed towards the window, showing off the wheels.

"You've got a car?" I said

"Picked it up yesterday," Richard replied.

I said, "never knew you could drive."

Richard responded, "a lot you don't know little man."

Rick's been helping my mum," Amanda said, "doing some handiwork and gardening for her."

"They need a man about the house, bro." said Richard confidently.

Rick? When did this all start? Why is Amanda calling my brother Rick? Since when did she know him like this, speak to him even? I had an urge to run out of the house, but I couldn't. I had to see this through. I had to find out what-was-what. If only Richard would go, I wanted to talk to Amanda alone, get some answers, the right ones, the ones that I desperately wanted to hear.

She said to Richard, "mum asked could you dig everything over down the end and then cut the grass, the lawnmower is in the shed."

"I can do that," Richard got up and stretched his long powerful limbs.

When he had gone out into the garden I said nervously, "this is a bit of a surprise."

"Rick you mean?" Amanda had her back to me, looking out of the kitchen window. "My mum just saw him hanging about and she wanted the place tidied up, she gives him £10 an hour."

"The last I heard about Richard was that he was working. How can £10 an hour take care of him and his lovely new car? Is that it, Amanda? He seems to be a man about the house, if you ask me." I still felt anxious, uncertain as to why Richard was here in Amanda's home, of all places. Just his presence was upsetting enough but what if there was more to it?

"How come he has a key to your house?" I asked.

She turned and looked at me, "why?"

I shrugged, "just asking."

Then Amanda said, "you been spying on me, do you think I'm seeing him or something?" There was an edge to her voice.

"No, of course not," I said.

"My mum gave it to him if you must know, I do go out. I can't stay here all the time, I can't wait in for people. I've got a life and I'm busy." Busy, that was Richard's word.

"Your mum obviously trusts him?" I said.

"Of course," Amanda replied.

"How did he get a car?" I asked.

"You joined the police or something?" she said sarcastically, "he earns money."

"Did he get signed for Chelsea while I was away then? You need to do a lot of gardening to buy a car and for driving lessons, I never knew he could drive."

"All of-a-sudden, you don't know much about your own brother, I always thought you two were close. You always used to stick up for him when you were kids, Rick might not be a premiership footballer, but he makes money Jason, he makes things happen." She shook her head at me as if she had said too much, she sat down at the table and began flipping the pages of a magazine.

I said, "listen do you want to go and see a film?"

"Don't mind," she said not looking up from the magazine.

I said, "What about this afternoon, 7 o'clock?"

"If you like," Amanda replied.

"Shall I come, round for you?"

Amanda said, "no, I'll meet you at the cinema, outside."

"OK, see you later then."

As I reached the front door Amanda called after me. "Jason…"

"What?"

Then Amanda said, "listen I'm sorry ok, I didn't know your brother was going to be here today, my mum didn't tell me."

I said, "sure, sure, so long as everything's OK between us." Pressing herself against me, Amanda said, "it is," and then she kissed me firmly on the lips, then quickly pulled away and closed the door behind her.

13

◼Destination Unknown

Amanda was waiting outside the cinema, seeing her wave to me, her green eyes lighting up, I began to relax for the first time that day. I guess she had felt awkward that Richard was there when I turned up at her house and that was why she had acted strangely with me. Now she seemed her old self again and it was just the two of us. We sat in the dark and held hands and kissed a bit. When the film started, she leant her head against my shoulder, it was magic, I didn't want to move. It was so good just to feel her warmth against me and hear her gentle sighing breath.

Afterwards we went for a coffee, there was so much I wanted to say to her, but the words just wouldn't come. Over the previous two weeks, I had built up a mental picture of how we would be together again, and now that moment was here, I felt tongue-tied and hardly spoke. Amanda was quiet too and sat staring out the window at people passing by. *Maybe this is what it's like, going out with a girl. You don't have to talk and do stuff all the time, you can just be together,* I thought to myself. I mustn't expect too much, I should just be cool about everything, but I couldn't stop making plans in my head.

"Do you want to go down to the sea one day?" I asked, then immediately thought, that must sound weird.

Amanda did one of her shrugs and said, "when?"

"Tomorrow if you like, we can get a train."

Amanda replied, "tomorrow?"

I said, "yeah."

"Where to", she said.

I replied, "Brighton?"

Then Amanda said, "I can't tomorrow."

"At the weekend then," I replied.

"Yeah, maybe," she said.

I said, enthusiastically, "we can go on the beach and then I enquired, do you like the sea?"

Amanda just shrugged her shoulders again.

I must sound stupid I thought, like some kid in an old-fashioned type of film or something. Shut-up Jason, I said to myself, shut-up or you're going to kill this stone dead, be cool or at least an adult.

"Ok," I said, "text me."

Amanda responded, "I can't, my phone was stolen remember."

"Will you be at church on Sunday?", I asked.

Amanda said, "no, I don't go now."

I asked, "what…why?"

Amanda sighed, "what's the point, all those people pretending they believe in God, just to try and look like they're better than everybody else."

I said, "I don't think that's true,… I used to think like that though."

Then Amanda said, "and you're saying you know better now then,…sorry, I didn't mean that."

I then said, "you've got to believe in something."

"I do," Amanda said.

"So, what is it?" I asked.

I was starting to enjoy our conversation now, it sounded like an argument, but it was a discussion and it was interesting. I wanted her to talk more like this, for us to really communicate.

"You wouldn't understand," she said, "I mean it's hard for me to explain, I've just moved on that's all."

I could hear echoes of the old Amanda talking, long before we got together—the sweet child with the green eyes and coffee-coloured skin, sitting on the steps outside her house telling me in a voice older than her years, what was right and what was wrong. But now what was right is now wrong and what was wrong is now right, everything seemed to have changed for her. I had the urge to make her explain, justify what she believed, or did she even know? Was it just her turn to play the rebel now, to turn away from God with nothing to put in His place?

I said, "I know it must be hard at home now, your dad gone and everything, but I'm sure your mum gets strength from the church."

"Does she?" Amanda looked annoyed and pained.

"I don't mean to pry," I said, "I know it's none of my business really."

"It doesn't matter," she said, and flashed me a bright reassuring smile but at the same time she looked restless, she finished her coffee and put on her jacket, "I'd better go."

I asked, "will your mum be home now?"

She nodded absently then stood up quickly, "look, sorry."

"For what?" I asked.

"I've got a lot going on that's all," she said.

I replied, "I know, well thanks for coming today, I'll walk back with you."

As we left the café, we decided to go for a walk but throughout the journey Amanda hardly spoke. We walked for what seemed like ages and hardly a word was spoken, then I heard a voice call out, "Mandy!" On the opposite side of the street was parked a shiny Mercedes sports car with tinted windows and standing beside it was a figure dressed in dark glasses and a leather jacket. I vaguely recognized him but couldn't place who it was at first, when I did my heart sank.

Amanda crossed the road and I followed, "you want a lift?" said Gareth.

My pulse quickening, I said, "no, she's going home."

I braced myself for a stream of abuse from Gareth, but instead he ignored me; it was as if I didn't exist.

"Remember that party I told you about?" he said to Amanda, "it's tonight, I can get you in." Party I thought, what party? And since when was she on speaking terms with Gareth? Richard's appearance had been a shock, was this a horrible nightmare? What had been going on while I was in Spain?

Amanda half-turned towards me and I sensed her awkwardness, there was a hollow feeling in the pit of my stomach. Then, his tone almost friendly, though still without looking at me, Gareth said, "he can come if you want."

Amanda shot me a sort of reluctant guilty look, unable to say anything and not quite knowing why I did so, I nodded. All I wanted, in that split second, was to please her and stay with her. A moment later we were in the back of the sports car, and before I could locate a seatbelt there was a squeal of tyres and the vehicle lunged forward into the center of the road. Gareth erupted in a wild, hysterical burst of laughter as he hit the accelerator for all it was worth. I saw the speedometer hit 40, 50 then hovering towards 70. The Mercedes was like a thunderbolt, jumping lights and scattering pedestrians as we tore through the honking traffic. As for where we were heading and what would happen to us that night, I had absolutely no idea.

14

◼ The Party

I exhaled as we finally swung into a driveway and the Mercedes skidded to a halt. I didn't recognise the place, Gareth had driven so fast we could be anywhere. Ahead of us was a big old house, the windows covered with metal security shutters. Several other smart looking cars were already parked outside. It didn't take long for my relief to give way to anxiety again. What should I do now, if I wandered off, I doubted I could find my way home. Besides I didn't want to leave Amanda's side, like a lamb to the slaughter, I followed her and Gareth into the house.

Loud, pulsating music shook the walls as we entered, my eyes hit by whirling lights that flashed out from darkened corners. There was a strong smell of weed. As the heavy door slammed shut behind me, I saw in the flashing lights a face I recognized.

"Hey little man," shouted Richard over the music.

"Hi," I replied.

Reading the uncertainty in my eyes, Richard grasped my arm and pulled me into the throng. I tried to turn back towards Amanda but could see no sign of her now. All around was a mass of bodies, some moving to the beat, others talking rapidly while some seemed to have frozen static, so stoned they could no longer form words or move. All they could do was grin like idiots. A voice came booming out over the microphone. It was Gareth, talking to the crowd and raising his arm in some kind of gesture of triumph. His words were indistinct, but some people seemed to understand, or at least approve and turned towards him echoing his posture. Richard had vanished. All I wanted now was to get out, but I couldn't go without…

"Jason!"

I spun round, Amanda was touching my shoulder, I found her, thank God! She guided me out of the room and into the hallway of the house where the noise was not quite so deafening. "Look, I'm sorry about this," she said, "I didn't expect to bump into Gareth tonight, but I felt I had to come, he's all right really."

"What do you mean?" I exclaimed in horror, "he is not all right!"

Amanda said, "OK, OK, I know, I know he does drugs and that, but well…"

"Well what," I said.

"He's a good person underneath," Amanda said.

I responded, "what kind of a person does drugs?"

Amanda retorted, "your mum for one."

I quickly said, "what?"

Amanda shockingly said, "I've seen her staggering down the road drunk."

I was furious and said, "that was ages ago and that wasn't drugs actually, it was alcohol, she was going through a rough patch!"

"All right, I'm sorry Jason, that was unfair of me, I'm just saying that you should give people a chance and not judge them. My dad was supposed to be a respectable person and then he walks out on us, what's Gareth done, that's so wrong?"

"Amanda he nearly got us killed on the way here and where do you think he got that car from, he doesn't even have a job."

Amanda, interjected and said, "how do you know,…there you go; judging people again! If you must know, Gareth's got his own business and he's helping your brother, you should thank him."

My head was spinning now, and it wasn't just the music. The only Gareth I knew and could see now, was the tough, frightening, couldn't-care-less Gareth; the one I had, for a brief period of my childhood, wanted to kill. Someone who commanded respect, but for all the wrong reasons. The person I had once plucked up the courage to fight against for my brother's sake; and now it seemed, the two of them were best mates. What about my lovely, beautiful girlfriend Amanda, what was it with her and Gareth, why was she now saying great things about Gareth, it was totally confusing.

Amanda was speaking to me again. "Alright, come on Jason, I can see you're uncomfortable here, do you want to go home?" Her words were just what I wanted to hear.

As we were about to leave, Gareth barged past us and opened the door while speaking into a mobile phone, "I can't get a signal, wait, wait! OK, I can hear you now." He went outside and walked towards the Mercedes, still talking. Was the car really his, I wondered? Some people were good at business I knew that—kids who'd made fortunes developing new apps and internet stuff. Maybe Gareth really was smart in a big way and perhaps Amanda was right about him. I sensed I had to try to understand her opinions, however disturbing I found them. I had to get my head round new possibilities if I wanted to keep her. Together we walked to the end of the driveway and around the corner. I desperately wanted to touch her now, just hold her hand and feel its tender warmth in mine again.

"Where are we?" I said.

"Don't worry, the bus stops just over there." As I looked to where she was pointing, I recognized where we were. It was strange, I must have been past this street loads of times but never once gone down there. I never even knew the big mysterious house was there. Lately, I seemed to be learning lots of new things about people as well as places. A bus came into view, "quick," Amanda said, "this one goes your way."

I began running, then realized she was not following, "come on," I called to her, "we'll miss it."

Amanda said, "you go, I've got to say goodbye to someone."

I asked, "who?"

Amanda said, "someone, I'll see you tomorrow, OK!" Amanda began to walk quickly back towards the house. As she came up the driveway she slowed down, Gareth was sitting on the bonnet of the Mercedes.

Gareth said, "hey, thought you'd run out on me."

"I wouldn't do that," said Amanda, "you know that."

"Not with a kid, eh," said Gareth.

Amanda shook her head, "not with anyone, I'm yours you know that."

Gareth smiled, "that's what I like to hear; now show me how much you are mine."

Amanda said, "what do you mean?"

"I think you know, come here," Gareth said.

Amanda stood still for a moment and Gareth repeated his command, with a harsh and uncompromising tone in his voice now, "I said come here!" Slowly, nervously she went closer and, in a lightening, move he reached out and grasped her hair in his fist and twisted it till she winced in pain, "oh, no, please Gareth, don't hurt me!"

Putting his face very close to hers, he said in a low purring voice, "hurt you? Why would I hurt you b****? I love you, don't I, so come, let's take a walk."

Still holding her hair in his vice like grip, he led her around the back of the old house, deep into the dense shrubbery.

As I sat on the bus, tears began to run down my face, I was so angry and upset. I didn't hear the bus conductor asking for my fare, he stood over me for a while then proceeded to take the fare of the other passengers and left me feeling very sorry for myself.

15

The Morning After

"Jason! Jason, let me in!"

L Lifting myself out of bed, my mind rearranged itself, shaking off the dream I had been in the middle of and the reassembling of events from the previous night. On getting home I must have fallen straight to sleep, my body and mind exhausted by the madness of the car ride, the crazy party and then Amanda suddenly abandoning me to go back there and now here she was banging on my front door.

"I'm coming, I'm coming," I called pulling on my clothes as I stumbled downstairs.

When I opened the door Amanda almost fell through into the hallway.

"Sorry, sorry, I had to see you," she said.

"What's wrong, are you, all right?" I asked, she looked exhausted, as if she had been crying a lot, with big blotches on her coffee coloured skin, her green eyes twitchy and anxious. I noticed she had on the same clothes as the night before.

"I'm OK, I'm OK, honestly," she said.

I then said, "you don't look it."

She snapped, "I said, I'm OK, alright! Sorry, sorry Jason, I need coffee, or something. Where's your mum?" I asked.

"At work, I slept in, looks like you didn't get any sleep at all, just saying." I added hastily and held up my hands before she could snap again.

We went into the kitchen and I made us some coffee, Amanda sipped hers and said nothing. The silence was like a heavy weight between us in the air, after a couple of minutes, I said, "So what happened at the party after I left?"

I felt her stiffen, looking down into her coffee cup she said casually, "nothing much to be honest, it was quite boring really, I don't know why I went back."

I then said, "you said you had to say goodbye to someone."

Amanda responded, "are you interrogating me again or what?"

I sighed, "no, no, just talking, I thought we were supposed to be going out that's all, and when people are going out, they talk to one another, share things. I don't want to hassle you though, so tell me to mind my own business. Now, do you want to do something together today; the two of us?"

Hearing myself speak I felt surprised by my manner, the way I was trying to handle the situation with confidence, it was all a front though; I knew that. Underneath I was unhappy, and worried by Amanda's behavior, the way she bit my head off every now and again without warning, and this admiration she seemed to have found for Gareth and his friends. Had last night killed it off though? Something had obviously gone on, maybe Gareth had been rude to her or something and she had now seen through him.

Amanda gave a deep sigh and a sort of anguished shudder, "if you must know, I wish I had never gone to that party."

I asked, "why, what happened?"

She bit her lip for a second and then suddenly began to cry, her shoulders heaving and great big tears rolling down her cheeks, her whole body was shaking.

I pulled my chair to her side and put my arm around her, "what's up, oh, my goodness, whatever is it Amanda…you know you can tell me, if it'll make things better."

"No, no!" she spluttered through her sobbing, "there's nothing anyone can do."

I said, "there must be something; just tell me, are you in some sort of trouble? If you are, I'm sure we can sort it out."

Amanda answered, "there's nothing to sort out; what's done is done."

"What has been done?" I asked.

She put her head in her hands and said, "I can't tell you, I can't tell anyone."

"Is it about your dad leaving?" I asked.

She was quiet for a moment then nodded and said, "I guess," she said hesitantly, "it's got something to do with that."

"You feel rejected, I understand," I said, but I'm here, I'm not saying I can ever take his place or make up for him leaving you, but I'm a friend; your best friend I hope."

Amanda lifted her tear-stained face and looked at me, her green eyes searching, pleading despairing almost. "Oh Jason, you're so young, so young and innocent."

I quickly said, "we're nearly the same age."

"I don't mean… oh what do I mean," she shook her head.

I said, "look, I know you might not think much of the idea, but why don't you start coming along to church again?"

She reached out a hand and stroked my face tenderly, I wanted to seize her in my arms and hold her tight at that moment, but I held back. "Poor little Bible basher," she murmured softly.

"Is that what you really think of me?" I asked

Amanda said, "no, no, no, but you've got to understand…"

I said, "what Amanda?"

"That God, well, He doesn't always have the answers, that's something I've learned from life," she said.

I asked, "have you tried asking Him?"

"You see that's just like you Christians!" She was exasperated now, "they always think they know best."

I said, "only the Lord knows best."

"There you go again", Amanda retorted.

This made both of us laugh, the tension suddenly released.

"OK," I said, "let's forget about God; for now, at least and let's plan what we're going to do today. What you need first is sleep, so why don't you take yourself up to the spare room and lie down? I'll get the house tidied up a bit and then later, I'll make us something to eat, how does that sound?"

Amanda nodded and yawned at the same time and said, "Ok boss man."

"Does your mum know where you are?" I asked.

"I don't think she really cares," Amanda replied.

"I'm sure she does, but I won't argue, no more arguing, deal," I said.

"Deal kid," Amanda said.

"Just don't start calling me kid," I said.

"I'm two years older than you," said Amanda

"Yeah, yeah, now get upstairs and sleep, do you want pizza for lunch?"

Amanda responded, "uh-huh."

While Amanda was upstairs sleeping, I sat in the quiet of the living room and prayed. I prayed that she would be happy and return to the Lord and that he would heal her heart. I prayed, selfishly, that she would also love me and that she and I would be together, in whatever way the Lord might see fit. I prayed for both her parents too, though I didn't quite know what I should wish for them. Last but not least, I prayed for my mum. That she would continue to find renewed strength and the kind of peace, which, as it says in the Bible, passes all understanding. I prayed that my brother Richard might not fall into further temptation and be one day delivered unto the Lord. As a Christian I knew I should pray for Gareth too, but it was something I wasn't willing to do, I was angry with him.

16

Suspicion

From then on Amanda and I spent almost every day together. My mum gave me some money and we did our trip down to Brighton, which was great. Amanda loved the crowded beaches and enjoyed listening to the musicians busting on their instruments. She said it was nice to be among such a lot of happy carefree strangers; as it made her feel happy too. Other days we caught the bus out into the countryside and walked along riverbanks and through beautiful woods and meadows. Amanda picked flowers and sang a lot; her sweet soulful voice reminding me of the first day I saw her—back when we were both so young. She didn't talk much about her parents; I thought it best not to ask. It was so good just to be with her now and I didn't want to risk spoiling the mood by raking up uncomfortable topics.

Neither did she speak of Gareth again. She was very reluctant to hang about the streets in our neighbourhood, and I guessed this was to avoid running into him. I was just relieved she had so suddenly got over whatever had made her see him as a hero. She did mention Richard briefly, saying he was no longer doing jobs for her mum. Although I was pleased about that, I was also curious as to why, but I didn't ask. The days we didn't go out of London, she insisted on spending indoors at my house or hers. On those occasions, she would be on edge, her expression would cloud over, and she would become testy and tearful. It was obvious she was feeling anxiety or regret about something. I assumed it was what she had told me: the sadness about her parents' break-up and that being at home reminded her of it all. But on-the-whole, her inner problems seemed to be easing and she was looking happier by the day; perhaps my prayers had helped.

The weeks passed quickly, the holidays would soon be over and the school year starting again. I wanted to make the most of what time we had left and tried to think of things Amanda would enjoy. I knew she was interested in art and after seeing a magazine article one day, I decided to surprise her with a visit to the National Gallery, which was only half an hour away on the train. Best of all, it was free to get in! We had arranged that she would call at my house that morning, so I would spring the surprise then. Just before she was due to arrive however, I heard a key in the door and my brother Richard appeared. He was dressed in new clothes and looked well and said, "how are you little man?"

I replied, "Oh, hi Rich! Ok, how're you doing?"

Richard said, "good, good, yeah, got my own business now, yeah." Even though I had seen him a few times in and around the area, it was several months since he had popped into what was now his old house. He paced around the room, checking the place out, leafing through some letters mum had left on the table.

"A business?" I said, "like Gareth?"

Richard looked at me and frowned, "I don't need other people you know."

I said, "no, no, I'm sure you don't."

Richard tone of voice now tensed, "I've got a mind of my own, a brain of my own, I make my own money."

"How did Gareth get to own that Mercedes?" I genuinely wanted to know.

"He doesn't own it," Richard smirked, "it's leased. Leasing is the way to go, we're in a similar kind of business if you must know."

"Doing what?" Again, I was genuinely curious, though nervous of what the answer might be.

Richard was quick to say, "buying and selling, music promotion, entertainments agency that kind of thing, you know, where's Mum by the way?"

I said, "at work of course."

Richard said, "what do you mean "of course"? How am I supposed to know?"

I shrugged, "sorry, it's just that she works two jobs now, how else do you think the bills get paid?"

Richard said, "ok, ok! No need to diss me."

I replied, "I wasn't, mum misses you, you know."

"Hmm," for a brief moment I saw a flicker of remorse in my brother's eyes. He sat down in the armchair, his expression more thoughtful, "all right kid," he sighed. "I know I've not been around a lot to help the family. You're right, you're right, but listen, I've been busy yeah, I'm an entrepreneur, it's not a nine-to-five job, know what I mean. Its 24/7 when you're in business."

I looked at the wall clock; Amanda was due any minute.

Richard continued, "but I'm going to make it up to you, to both of you; very soon. I've got plans you know, I've got a big deal coming off, which could get us a bigger house. You'd like that; and what about a car for you, learn to drive, eh?"

He so obviously wanted me to be pleased and impressed that I nodded enthusiastically. "WOW, Yeah, great Rich!"

He was so glad about my response, his face cracking into a gleeful smile, "ok, ok, good". Then he said, "now, I've got to talk to you about the girl."

"Girl?" I felt a quiver of anxiety run through me, "you mean Amanda?"

Richard continued to ask, "how many girls you got? Just the one if I know you, but how much do you know about her Jason?"

"What do you mean? I know everything about her," I said.

Richard was quick to add, "no-one knows everything about anyone."

"What are you getting at?" I asked.

"Ok well it's like this, she's not what you might call an innocent girl."

"What are you saying?" I said.

Then he said, "I'm saying like, you might not be the only one bro."

I felt as if the floor was swaying beneath me and I was going to keel over, "what? You're lying," why, why are you saying this Rich?"

"Just so you know, because you're my brother, and we gotta stick together against the enemy, whether it's the law, or the government, or whoever tries to ★★★★ us over."

"Enemy, what are you talking about?" I was angry with him now, incensed that he dared to spread these horrible lies and ruin my happiness. "How dare you! I love Amanda and she loves me."

"Oh boy," Richard shook his head, "I knew this was going to be bad." His tone was not mocking, but it did not need to be, my own words had been enough. Instantly I hated myself for speaking them. Oh why, why, why had I declared my love so openly, so publicly, even if only to my brother? Or perhaps especially to him? It would now be my own fault if all that I cherished in the world was to crumble and die.

17

Holding On

I struggled to stay calm. It was difficult to think clearly. OK, if Amanda had dated other boys at some time or other, was this such a terrible thing? And it was still a big if. Richard's exact words had been "you might not be the only one," which was not an accusation of anything. Perhaps he had just seen her talking to someone, having a laugh with them. Maybe at the party that night; and thought he ought to tell me about it. Rich was a thief and a liar and didn't have much sense of responsibility. But he did have certain principles, and would as he said, look out for me that way. I felt sure of it. Most likely he was just being over-protective, nothing more. Hey, it was something to feel good about; that I had an older brother who, for all his faults, was fiercely loyal to me. I've overreacted, panicked for no reason, I told myself I should show my gratitude towards him.

"Thanks for telling me this Rich," I said, "I really appreciate it, Amanda's all right though, honestly."

"Bro, I think you ought to…"

Whatever Richard was about to say next was interrupted by a knock on the door. "Hi Jason! How are you and how've you been?" she whispered gently after kissing me on the cheek "Rick! This is a surprise." Amanda had just walked into the room, he was smiling a tense, apprehensive kind of smile. "I - didn't know you were here Rick, how… how are you doing?"

Richard cast his eyes down and murmured softly, "I'm good, yeah, I'm good." Then before anyone else could speak he stood up decisively and said to me, "I'll call you later, little man," and slipped deftly out of the room. A few seconds later, we heard his car start up and the screeching of tires as it sped away.

There was silence for a moment as Amanda looked at me warily, then she said, "what did he want?"

"He just came to see me," I said.

"I gathered that, but I thought he'd sort of left home, why has he turned up now?"

"Why not?" Worrying thoughts were still rumbling through my head, but this question made me want to defend Richard in a way I hadn't felt for a long time. "Well, this is technically still his home, too."

"Yeah of course, sorry, it's just that, well, I thought… I thought…" Then there was a long pause as Amanda looked at me, "why would he just suddenly show up like that?"

"We get on as a family, he is my brother you know! Not long ago you were acting like his best mate, saying how great he was. Have you changed your mind about him again?"

Amanda's coffee-coloured skin seemed to darken, was she blushing I wondered? Ignoring my question, she said, "was he talking about me?"

I was about to say "yes" then hesitated, my impulse was to tell the truth, but I also wanted to know the truth. Had Richard simply seen Amanda talking to some other boy and felt annoyed on my behalf, or was there something more I should know about?

I asked, "why do you think he was talking about you?"

She shuffled her feet awkwardly, "I don't know, just the way he looked when I came in just now; then running out like that. You looked like the two of you just had an argument."

Should I confront the issue I wondered; tell her straight out what Richard had said and see what her reaction would be?

But I knew at the same time that this would show my mistrust, crack the beautiful friendship, and yes—the love between us. I could not let that happen. instead I answered her question with a half-truth, "we sort of had an argument, yeah."

Amanda asked, "what about?"

"Our mum working long hours every day, and him not being around, but it was cool because he said, he's going to help us out with money soon."

Amanda quickly asked, "what money?"

"From his business, I guess, yeah, he wants to help."

"Oh, good," hearing this Amanda seemed to relax, she put her bag down and sat on the sofa. "So, what are we going to do today?"

I had almost forgotten about my surprise, "I thought we could go up to the National Gallery, if you want."

Her face lit up, "yeah, OK, that's really cool."

I said, "great, OK then, want a coffee first?"

"Yeah, all right."

"Oh, and I found this article about the gallery," I handed her the magazine then went into the kitchen and put the coffee on. As I was finding the cups I said, "listen um, can I ask you a serious question?"

"Yeah what?" Amanda said, not looking up from the magazine.

I hesitated for a moment then said, "well, what I need to know is -"

"For goodness sake, what? Amanda said.

"Do you… do you take sugar?"

"What are you going on about?" she laughed, "you know I don't."

"Oh yeah, of course, OK, that's um, good then."

I never had it in me to ask her about her relationship with Gareth, but I was desperate to get to the bottom of it all.

18

At the Cross Road

"Come on Jason, you'll be late!"

"I'm coming Mum, for goodness sake."

"Don't use the Lord's name in vain."

"I said goodness."

"Never mind, just get in the car, you don't want to be late for school on the first day back."

The autumn term had started, and I couldn't believe the holidays were over so soon. During the last week I had seen nothing of Amanda. She'd said she was desperate to get a good start for the new year ahead as it was her last year at secondary school. She was spending every day at the town library. It gave me a chance to get my own holiday stuff done, although I had been tempted to go and see her at the library every day.

Now I couldn't wait to make up for lost time. "It's only twenty past eight, and I'm going to get there far too early. Why can't I walk like I always do?"

My mum was already in the car with the engine running. "Hush, I'm going that way to work so I'll drop you; you'll see Amanda soon enough." I fastened my seatbelt and said nothing. Obviously, it was common knowledge that Amanda and I were going out. "I'm glad you're seeing her, she's a nice girl," my mum said, as she stopped at the junction with the main road. Then she said, "a pity she doesn't come to church anymore though, perhaps you can encourage her to come back?"

"I'll try," I said.

"Oh look, there she is now, but…" mum pointed across the road with an expression of puzzlement. Amanda stood on the corner talking into her phone, she was wearing torn jeans and a tracksuit top. "It's the start of term, it can't be a non-uniform day today can it, Jason?"

"No, no I don't think it is mum."

"She must have got the start date wrong then, we'd better let her know so she can quickly go home and change." My mother wound down the window and leaned out, at that moment, another car pulled up opposite and Amanda got in.

My mum laughed, "looks like she's already realized and phoned home, I didn't know her mother had a Mercedes though."

"She hasn't, look Mum, can you please let me out here? Please!"

"What? Oh, all right, all right, out you get but go straight to school and mind the road, I love you," she blew me a kiss.

"Love you Mum."

I was already out of the car and crossing over towards the Mercedes, recognizing Gareth's number plate, my heart racing. I walked forward, hardly knowing what I was doing, I rapped on the tinted window. As the driver's door opened, I waited for Gareth's face to appear, a torrent of abuse, a fist to hurtle towards me. Instead, it was my brother staring at me.

"Jason?"

"What are you doing Rich," I said bemused, "I thought this was Gareth's car?"

"It is, he's busy now, so he lent it to me."

"Why?" I said.

Richard looked away, "to like, pick up Mandy."

"What do you mean pick her up? She's going to school."

"You're behind the times little man, I tried to explain it to you and now I'm defo going to tell you all about your precious, Amanda."

"Explain what? What are you on about Richard?"

"Leave it Rich, I will tell him," Amanda blurted out, "I've left school if you must know Jason." Amanda got out of the car, "I am not going back to school."

"You don't have to do this Mandy," Richard said.

Amanda said to Richard, "what are you saying?"

"I'm saying, you don't have to come with me to Gareth's now. You don't have to see him again if you don't want to. You can go back to school and carry on going out with Jason. It's clear that he loves you, just swear to me you'll never tell Gareth I said that. I'll tell him you've changed your mind that's all."

I felt dizzy with confusion and shock the noises and fumes of the rush hour traffic along with my racing thoughts, were making my head spin. "Amanda," I said. "Will you please tell me what's going on?" Of course, I probably knew what was going on now. That was why my voice was shaking and I thought I might faint at any minute.

Then Amanda said, "Jason look I'm really sorry, but it's like this, when you were away in Spain, I got sort of friendly with Gareth."

Hearing this from her own lips, I could feel myself wanting to cry, but had to be strong. I just wanted to run away—run and never see her again.

Suddenly, I couldn't even bear the sound of her name in my head, let alone say it out loud. But something kept me rooted to the spot, wanting to hear her spell out the awful ugly truth that had already hit me like a sledgehammer.

Feigning stupidity, I said, "friendly… in what way?"

Amanda said, "friendly, you know."

I responded with "no, I don't know, tell me."

"Well the point is he's got himself in some trouble, and he needs my help right now, he needs a friend."

I said, "he's got Rich, he doesn't need you."

Richard said, "I've told her that, man…all I said to Gareth was that I'd come and ask you… you make up your own mind."

I stared at Richard, "so whose side are you on?"

"I'm not on anyone's side little man, I'm just saying, I know you two are an item, or you were, I don't know. I'm trying to look out for you here." He ran his hands through his hair. "The main thing is she doesn't have to go to Gareth just because he clicks his finger. But like I say, that is between the three of us, he doesn't know yeah?"

"Yeah, yeah, OK," I said, "please, Amanda can we talk?"

She looked away, I couldn't tell if there were tears in her eyes or if the traffic fumes were making them water, Gareth is wanted by the police," she said, "he's gone into hiding up in Manchester."

My upset suddenly spilled over into burning indignation now, "why am I supposed to care?"

Amanda said, "I'm just telling you, I have to go to him."

"Why, you're just 15 years old and your leaving home, leaving school to go to Manchester, what about your mum?" I was trying hard not to break down and cry right there in front of them both. "I don't get it, what has happened to you? Why can't things be like they used to be between us? What does Gareth have to do with you, with us?"

Amanda seemed impatient and said, "do I need to spell it out?"

I shook my head, "no!" I knew now what had happened at the party in the summer. Perhaps I had always known, I felt pathetic, useless, stupid. I felt a sharp pain that was so intense, so awful that I wanted to be free from it, but for some reason, I was unable to move.

"Gareth is strong Jason, in a way that you aren't, I don't just mean physically strong, he makes things happen. You're a nice person but nice people don't do it for me, life with him is exciting."

I said, "what, you think being a criminal is exciting?"

Amanda was quick to give her opinion, "if you must know, yes, and what do you mean by criminal? Governments commit crimes, bankers commit crimes, priests commit crimes."

"He can't be that smart if he's got to go on the run." Even as I spoke those words, I thought, what was the point of arguing about it? As if there was something to win, to prove? I had lost her and lost my dignity, I was in the mire, so why wallow in it.

Amanda looked at me with a mad, unrepentant expression, her eyes now gleaming with pride and defiance, "he'll get out of it don't worry, he's got nine lives, he'll live forever."

I said, "only God can grant the gift of eternal life."

She uttered a horrible laugh, the ugliest sound I had ever heard, "there you go again, giving me more Bible quotes, maybe you should become a preacher!"

"Maybe I will, God will not abandon you if only you will ask for his help"

"WOW! That's so attractive. NOT! Listen, my dad promised he would never let me down, and what happened? He walked out on me."

"I'm sorry about that, truly I am, but Gareth is not the answer Amanda, however strong and tough you might think he is. Don't judge his character by how many people are scared of him. He won't stand by you when you need him the most."

Amanda added, "he already has."

"Why do you say that?"

Amanda shouted as she hastily jumped back into the car, "look just leave me alone alright!

"If you must know he took my virginity and I am pregnant!"

19

~~~~~~

■ Pain

What happened immediately after Amanda dropped her bombshell became rather hazy in my memory. Richard exchanged some very heated words, towards her and then the next minute, the Mercedes was roaring away up the road and I stood there in pain. Crying to myself, my heart was broken. I couldn't go to school and had to turn back.

"Having his baby!" I said to myself, she was still fifteen, she was too young.

I couldn't tell my mum that I had bunked off school and put on a brave face when she came home that evening.

The days and weeks that followed, went by in a blur. Some mornings I awoke having forgotten all about what had happened, as if it had been a bad dream, only for the reality to crash in on me again. Each time, like a punch in the stomach. My mum knew immediately that something had gone seriously wrong in my life and soon realized that Amanda was not a name to mention in my presence. The few times she had tried talking to me about it, was either met by a flood of tears or me storming off angrily. I was shy of telling anyone the details, partly because it seemed not right to betray what may have been told to me in confidence. But largely out of not wishing to confront the fact that I was dumped so horribly. I also felt that weird sense of shame at someone else's crime or sin against me. Everything was now spoiled and at times, I felt as if I just wanted to die. Though it was very hard to see any kind of happiness or peace of mind ever again, I had to try to believe in it. Only the Lord could see me through this dark time and each day I prayed for guidance, and I always prayed for Amanda too. I dared not hope she would ever return to me. How could either of us ever turn back the clock after something like this?

I'd assumed Amanda had gone to Manchester to be with Gareth and I wondered whether I would ever see her again. But as time went by, I became increasingly doubtful. Then one day about six months later, quite out of the blue, I did. She was coming out of a shop on High Street. Turning in my direction she stopped and stared for a second, then came over. I stared too, her appearance had changed, not in a good way. Her jeans, leather jacket and trainers all looked expensive, top of the line. But she seemed painfully thin. Her cheekbones were prominent, and her once clear green eyes were clouded and sunken deep into their sockets.

"Hi Bible Basher!" she said cockily, did she even realise how unwell she looked I wondered? "How's God these days?"

"Hmm, how are you?" I asked. It felt odd, like I was talking to a stranger. Was this the same bright, thoughtful, caring girl I had held hands with whilst walking on the seashore? The one who used to tell the bad boys off at school. Was it the same girl who everyone said had a great future ahead of her? A future that in those days of blissful innocence, I dreamed I would be sharing?

"Good yeah, everything's good, Gareth got off the charges, so we're back for a bit. He's down here for a few days on business, then we're going back to Manchester."

Suddenly a throbbing bass beat exploded into the air at the same time I felt something hard bump against my leg from behind; almost knocking me over, I spun around. The bonnet of a car had mounted the pavement, "eh, watch where you're going!"

I shouted instinctively, I hadn't recognized the car. It was a shiny black Mercedes convertible, with its hood down, showing off the lush leather interior and gleaming dashboard, I was nearly run over by it. "Get back to school Bible Boy," growled Gareth over the pulsing music, "and stop hassling my woman, unless you want to get hurt."

"I'm not afraid of you," I said feeling very afraid and walking around to face him as he sat in the car.

"Who-ooh!" Gareth jeered, the next second, he had opened the driver side door hard, slamming it against my knee. I winced in pain and staggered back, only to feel something smash into my chin, sending me keeling over onto the pavement. When I got to my feet Gareth was back in the car with Amanda beside him. The bass beat thumping again, the Mercedes roared into life and shot off out of sight.

"Are you alright Jason?"

"Eh?" I turned to see a girl I knew from my school looking at me with concern.

"There's blood coming from your mouth," she handed me a tissue.

I said, "thanks."

"You should report that, it's actual bodily harm, I'll be a witness," she said.

"Oh, no, it's OK, I asked for it really."

The girl said, "I'm sure you didn't, that girl used to go to our school, didn't she?"

"Yeah, she did."

"Such a shame, and I recognize that boy too, Gareth, wasn't it? He was excluded for selling drugs and fighting ages ago. Someone said he did time, didn't you used to go out with that girl?"

I said, "sort of."

"What do I mean sort of?"

"Of course, I went out with Amanda," I said as I wiped the blood from my mouth, my voice shaking, "she was my soul mate, I actually loved her, and I still do."

The girl looked at me and said, "are you sure you're, alright?"

"Yes, yes thanks," I said.

"Well," she said, "you know where to find me if you do want a witness, or anything else."

I said, "yeah, sure."

"Strange though, isn't it?"

"What?" I said.

"To think we're still at school and she's, well, you know," she gestured vaguely at where the Mercedes had driven off.

"Yes," I said, the tears welling in my eyes, "it is quite strange."

20

◼Rescue Attempt

I felt torn apart, just when I might have been turning a corner, when the passage of time could have begun to heal my wounds and let me forget about Amanda, those wounds had been opened again. Seeing her gaunt, unhealthy features had affected me deeply. Her conceited, contemptuous manner had been unable to hide her insecurity and unhappiness. Up until that moment, to my shame but as a way coping, I suppose, a part of me had begun to hate her. Now seeing her so hollow and worn down and frayed at the edges, while trying to act glib and cheerful as if everything was normal, I was hit by a different feeling entirely. With a painful, aching tenderness, I pitied Amanda. I realized that the girl with the green eyes and coffee coloured skin, still meant so much to me. And the punch in the mouth from Gareth had sharpened that pity into an angry determination to help her. He was a bully who had taken her away and obviously ruled her life now. But why should he be allowed to carry on doing so?

Yet I had to admit my feelings were still rather mixed up. Although jealousy had tempted me to loathe her at one point, if she came running back would I not want to take her back? Perhaps. Our emotions are a strange phenomenon, which can sometimes make our lives very difficult. Our emotions may hinder us from separating love from jealousy, pride, vanity and all the other faults we are prone to.

The one thing I was sure of though, whatever my motives were. I wanted to get Amanda away from Gareth, but could it be done? Despite everything, there was it would seem, a part of her that still liked him. Or probably respected him or felt proud of being his girlfriend. How could I possibly persuade her this was foolishness and that she should leave him? There was perhaps an element of fear too; of what he might do to her if she tried to walk out on him. If I tried to talk to her about the Lord, she would probably only sneer at me again, with that snide, false confidence she put on. I realized that I had to give her a very strong reason to turn away from Gareth of her own accord. The problem was, I just couldn't think of one, then quite unexpectedly I got my chance. It was the following Saturday, I was coming back from the High Street with some shopping for my mum, when I noticed Gareth's Mercedes parked a little way down a side street. This time the hood was up, I was about to walk on when I saw the car door open and a girl got out. It wasn't Amanda though, it was someone I had never seen before. Tucking myself against a fence, I watched as the girl lowered her head back towards the car. Gareth's head then leaned out and the two of them embraced, sharing a long, slow, sensual kiss. I froze against the fence as the girl waved to Gareth and began walking quickly towards me, heading for High Street. As she passed, I saw she was very beautiful and realized with a shock how much she reminded me of Amanda—but Amanda the way she used to look, perhaps only a few months ago.

With my heart beating fast I hurried back home, dropped off the shopping and ran straight round to Amanda's house. What made me think she would be there I don't know but as soon as I knocked on the door, she appeared. She looked a bit better than the previous time I had seen her, with her hair tied back, cheeks fuller and glowing and her green eyes with more of their old luster. The smile she gave me was more like the Amanda I had always known. The thought flashed immediately through my head that she and Gareth had split up, this was why she was back home now. But what on earth should I say to her?

Amanda said, "hi Jason."

I responded, "hi! I thought you might be here."

Amanda said, "uh-huh," she looked at me curiously now.

"I just saw Gareth," I said.

"Oh?" Amanda responded.

I replied, "with that other girl."

Manda said, "what other girl?"

I said, "um, I'm not sure…his new girlfriend I guess," I felt uncertain again now.

She folded her arms and glared at me suspiciously and said, "what do you mean?"

"I saw them kissing just now, she was getting out of his car, just off High Street, ou mean you don't know?"

Amanda's eyes glared, and her jaw set tight and yelled, "you little trouble-maker! I knew you were a goody two shoes, but I didn't think you were a stirrer as well. Get the hell out of here, NOW, before I ring Gareth and tell him what you're up to. Trying to split us up!" Her eyes filled with rage now, she came forward onto the doorstep and swung her foot hard, catching me on the thigh.

"I thought you ought to know that's all," I protested backing away, "we were friends once, more than friends I thought, I owed it to you."

"The only thing you owe me," she snarled, "is to keep your stinking little Bible bashing nose out of my business. Now get out of here!" She came towards me again and carried on kicking me all the way down the steps and onto the pavement. After she had closed the door, I heard sobbing coming from within.

Desperate to talk to Amanda that evening, I found her old phone number that she had previously given to me, I called it. To my surprise she picked up, "it's Jason, listen, I wasn't trying to cause any trouble today honestly. The last thing I want to do is mess things up for you more than they… sorry. I meant, perhaps I got the wrong end of the stick."

Amanda said, "yeah you did."

I said, "I'm sorry I upset you."

"You didn't upset me," she said.

"It's just that I saw what I saw, but as I say, maybe I got it wrong."

Amanda retorted, "whatever."

"Well, sorry, anyway, how are you?" I said.

"Fine, I'm going back to Manchester next week, my mum doesn't know but she really doesn't care anyway."

"With Gareth?" I enquired.

"Of course."

"Oh OK, Amanda", I said, "could I ask you one favour before you leave?"

"My name's Mandy."

OK, Mandy."

Then Amanda said, "What favour?"

"Would you come to church with me on Sunday?"

I heard her sigh heavily, "I think you know the answer to that, Jason you're a bright kid, but when are you going to grow up and get it into your skull that the only person who helps you is yourself? Not God or Jesus or priests or vicars, the only person I ever trusted was my dad. He made me a promise he would never leave me, he said I was his princess, like in a fairy tale. Well that fairy tale has turned out to be my nightmare, it's a load of ★★★★!" she swore. "So now I don't trust anyone, least of all the church or anything to do with it."

"Except for Gareth," I said.

Amanda said, "What?"

"I said, you trust Gareth."

There was silence for a second then the phone went dead.

Next morning, I awoke early and went straight to Amanda's house. It was Saturday, and although it was a long shot, I was determined to somehow persuade her to come out with me for the day. Anywhere. I would suggest an art gallery then tomorrow, we might even go to church. *If at first you don't succeed,* I repeated to myself over and again as I walked, *try, try and try again.*

Putting on my most cheerful smile I knocked at the door, as it opened the smile froze on my face, for standing there was Gareth.

"Well, well," he said.

I was about to turn and run then said, "is Amanda in?"

He glared at me for a moment, "come in," nervously I entered the house and heard the door shut behind me.

"Well, well," he said again, "quite the little detective aren't we. Except you've been telling lies, lies about me." He slapped his chest with his fist, I looked down, not daring to meet his eyes. "Mandy told me what you said to her. She even started accusing me, till I put her right. Don't they teach you not to lie at Bible class?" He began to pace around me menacingly and said "Thou Shalt Not Lie?"

"Sorry, I just wanted to have a quick word with Amanda," I said meekly.

Gareth interjected, "you've had enough quick words, now I'm…"

There was a rustle of clothing on the stairs and Amanda appeared, seeing her face, I gulped. Her cheeks were bruised and cut, her eyes puffy and swollen.

"Oh my god!" she said, "it's you!"

"I'm just setting him straight Mandy," Gareth said, "go back upstairs."

Out of concern I said, "Amanda, what happened to you?"

"I've got you to thank for this," she said touching her damaged face, "you and your *******" she began to swear. "…Bible bashing interfering, just get out and leave us alone!"

Gareth snarled raising his hand towards her, "I said, go back upstairs woman."

"Leave her alone!" I yelled rushing between them.

The next second, Gareth's hand had closed into a fist and connected with my nose. As I reeled, he seized me by the shoulders, manhandled me from the room and threw me out of the house, the front door slammed shut.

I staggered a safe distance up the road and sat down on a step, blood trickling from my nose. My head was throbbing, my mind in turmoil, I tried to think about what to do next. I knew I should report the assault, and the fact that Gareth had obviously used violence against Amanda. But if nothing could be proved, might that not put her in more danger from him? If the police could just go and arrest Gareth and take him out of her life forever, she would be free, but was it as simple as that?

21

Several Years later

As things turned out, I would not get the chance to find out how simple or complicated anything would be. Not that day nor the next, nor for a long time to come. Looking back, I can recall every detail of what happened on the afternoon after Gareth threw me out of Amanda's house.

Well, time had passed. I was now much older, twenty-five years old to be precise. I hardly saw or heard from Amanda, other than the times when she would spend the odd day or two at her mother's house. But things were never the same. She and I would meet up occasionally to catch up but she always seemed nervous around me. Her conversations always centered around how terrible her life had turned out. What used to get me was that shortly after Amanda arrived, you could set your watch on Gareth's timely appearance and how quickly the two of them would drive off to Manchester. And each time it felt as though she had no say in the matter. On what seemed like Amanda's last visit, I remember walking past her house and seeing someone in the front garden putting up a "For Sale" sign. The next minute a large van appeared, and two men entered the house and began carrying furniture out.

I realized with a sudden rush of sadness that this was the mirror image of the scene I had witnessed a long, long time ago, when Amanda and I were both still children and her family had just moved in. Her father had still been there with his "Princess," telling her he loved her and would never go away. This time though, the furniture was being taken out and not brought in. Her father was long gone and Amanda herself was nowhere to be seen. As I stood and watched, Amanda's mum appeared, seeing me, she did not smile. "I'm leaving now too Jason," she called out in a rather sad tone. "My life has been shattered and now I have no-one. As for Amanda, she left years ago as you know. Gone I tell you, gone, but don't ask me where. With no address, no clues as to where she was, what could I do? After calling her several times, trying to reach out to her and getting no reply, I gave up trying."

During this long period, unsurprisingly some major changes took place in my own life. Amanda must be at least twenty-seven years now. WOW! How quickly time flies.

After leaving school I went to college, then university and graduated with a first in Wealth Management. I'd started a great job, which afforded me to leave home and purchase a flat of my own not too far from mum's, I drove a nice shiny BMW, too. The family house had been sold as it was way too big for the two of us and my mum had downsized, which helped with my deposit. The church was still at the heart of who I was, it's faith and fellowship the bedrock of a happy and harmonious existence. I had never understood why, after the truth had come out about Amanda and Gareth, that every time I saw or even thought about her, she would make me either freeze, boil with anger or simply cry. I had asked myself the question more than once before, but would I ever see her again? That, like so many things, was in the hands of the Lord.

The time was approaching for one of our church's annual events; a week of revival, which included a guest speaker. It was my responsibility to make sure he was well looked after. Our revival services were always special, an important part of the calendar that no-one liked to miss. Friday night was the opening night, this year our guest was to be a Reverend Edward Nelson, a dynamic and anointed speaker, who was well sought after, always with a good or guiding word for someone. Hence, we felt especially privileged to welcome him. Focused and ready for my forthcoming tasks and duties, I was looking forward to the coming week, although nothing could have quite prepared me for what was about to happen during the course of it.

The opening night was fantastic! The worship service was breath-taking, totally awesome and the presence of God filled the sanctuary. People were bowing before God, they were singing, they were clapping their hands, they were dancing, they were crying; it was more than special. Anyone who had ever attended one of our revival services will know exactly what I mean. But something else occurred that night which took my breath away. As the Reverend, who had been preaching with great inspiration began drawing to a close, he said to us, "you know, there are three types of people that come into your life, those that come for a season, those that come for a reason, and those that come for life. Sometimes God must shift certain people out of your life for a season, and some of these people he has shifted, he then prepares to bring them back at the right time."

This was great preaching I thought but saw no relevance to myself. It was then that the Reverend pointed straight at me and said. "Son, there was someone whom you were fond of, who is coming back into your life." In a flash it dawned on me, he meant Amanda! But alas, I thought, he must surely be wrong. Perhaps someone had told him that Amanda was once a big part of my life, and what had happened to her had grieved me ever since. It was therefore a kind gesture to tell me her "season" had changed again, and she was "coming back" to the church and to a wholesome, happier and more fulfilling life, following the ways of God.

But I didn't believe it, I remembered the one thing she had been sure about was that she wanted nothing to do with God. She had blamed him for everything that had gone wrong in her life. It would indeed take a miracle for Amanda to walk into church now. The thought of what she and other people might say or do in that situation, made me feel quite uncomfortable. However, I didn't see it as the least bit likely to happen and the Reverend had to be mistaken.

Nevertheless, I had very mixed feelings, all my deepest anxieties and regrets about Amanda had been stirred up again. On the way home, I was starting to wish, with all my heart, that the Reverend's prophecy would come true. And yet, my soul ached with what I was convinced must be a false and forlorn hope.

22

◾An Unexpected Visitor

That night, as always, before retiring I had a cup of tea. I prayed, read my Bible then fell asleep, but then something unusual occurred. I had a dream about Amanda—something that hadn't happened in years. It was all quite strange and surreal, and I couldn't make sense of it. Was I being asked to do something? Was she in trouble and calling out to me? Or could it be a test of my faith. Was I desiring her? The dream had not been that explicit.

On that Saturday evening our guest speaker was due to preach again. I had just collected him from his hotel and was driving to the church, when passing a bus stop and with complete shock, I thought I saw Amanda standing there. Checking my rear-view mirror, it seemed I had been mistaken. Then suddenly came a sense of déjà vu. I had seen her in this same place in my dream the night before. My heart started to race, and I kept telling myself it could not be true. My mum was next to me in the passenger seat and the Reverend sat behind, looking meaningfully into my eyes each time I glanced in the mirror. Struggling to focus on the road ahead, I began to wonder if he knew something I did not. Then as he caught my eye again, he said, "God works in mysterious ways, does He not son?"

Throughout the whole service I couldn't concentrate. I just kept thinking about Amanda, praying that it was her I had seen and that for whatever reason, she was coming to church. Every so often, my eyes searched her out amongst the congregation. It was difficult to know who was and wasn't there because the church was packed, as it always was for revival week. At the close of service an altar call was made, but with no sign of Amanda my heart sank. It was then I realized how much I had been looking forward to seeing her.

Mum wanted to stay behind at the church to attend to a few things, so I offered to take the Reverend back to his hotel first and collect her later. As it was just the two of us in the car, I began to share with him my dream of the night before and speculating on what it might mean. I even ventured to talk a little about Amanda's life, including the part I had once played in it and how I had got it into my head that she might turn up, especially after what he had said to me in the service the previous day. The Reverend looked at me for a moment then said, "Son, you will see your little princess again," my jaw dropped. Although I had never spoken to Amanda in those terms, the name, which she had once told me her father used to call her, had certainly been how I thought about her many times. But how could the Reverend know this, he was beginning to freak me out.

Revival week meant that all our regular church activities were suspended, but reluctant to miss our usual Wednesday Bible study, I had invited some friends and church family around to my house, my mother was there as well. The plan was to read and discuss the scriptures as usual, share a bite to eat and enjoy an uplifting and convivial evening. At 8.00 PM we had just opened our Bibles and begun to read, when there was a knock at the door. We exchanged curious glances, all those who'd been invited were already here so who could it be? Sister Bernice's eyes then lit up, through a mouthful of her favourite bourbon biscuits, she burbled excitedly, "Oh, it'll be my friend Amanda! I've been witnessing to her on-and-off, she was living in a hostel you know and then she went missing. But lo and behold, she turned up again out of the blue! I knew you wouldn't mind me inviting her to join us tonight, Jason, you don't mind, do you?"

Even without a mouthful of biscuits, I was speechless, did I mind? The Reverend's words rang in my head, "God works in mysterious ways doesn't He Son?" Laying down my Bible I couldn't get up from the table quick enough and had to make a conscious effort to keep my emotions in check. My mum had a way of knowing what I was thinking before I even thought it. A gene I was convinced was inherent in all women. Almost exploding with joy and apprehension in equal measure, I threw open the door and there she was, my long-lost friend with the pretty green eyes, I stared at her, speechless.

Amanda laughed, those wondrous green eyes sparkling, "you haven't changed, much, have you?" I continued looking straight into her eyes, mesmerised by her sheer beauty. She had certainly changed, she not only looked healthy but there was a glow about her, a kind of radiant light surrounding her. Only Amanda had ever had this effect on me and after all these years, I thought I had grown out of it, obviously not.

"Close your mouth, Jason," she giggled, "stop gawking at me like that and let me in please."

"Oh, yes, sorry, Amanda please come in," I gestured towards the others, who smiled welcomingly. She entered, greeted everyone amiably and took a seat opposite me. There was so much I wanted to say to her, to ask her. Where had she been? What had she been doing? A hundred and one questions but right now, the Bible class had to begin.

Amanda took to the proceedings with earnest enthusiasm, doing her fair share of snacking and drinking as she listened to the readings; all the while nodding and smiling. When she read, or joined in the discussions, it seemed like she really knew her Bible. Her former hostility to all things religious, now quite the reverse. I sat in amazement, struggling to focus my attention on the class. Every time she spoke or even raised her head, I had to look away, as smitten as the shy adolescent I had once been with her. All sorts of analogies began to flash into my mind. She was the caterpillar that had turned into a butterfly, the diamond in the rough that had now been polished and gleamed with God's love, the vein of precious gold prized from the earth to shine with new life and shower her fellow human beings with light and joy.

For me, and I felt everyone present, she was almost like a sweet and fragrant perfume, a sacred incense that had entered our midst, God had beautified Amanda. No longer was she wearing the garment of heaviness but instead God had clothed her in a garment of praise. He had taken all her mourning and had turned it into the oil of joy. Clearly, she was now recognising, for herself, that she was, fearfully and wonderfully made; God loved her and accepted her with all her faults. This surely was the secret of her newfound confidence. Gone was the strident, embittered tone that had taken a hold of her and in its place was a quiet confidence, yet with a voice modulated and kind and a willingness to listen to others. It was the Amanda I had fallen in love with all those years ago. She was back; Oh, joy of joys!

Still, I had to steady myself, to be aware of being carried away by my emotions. I needed to try and separate my pleasure in her renewal, from any other kind of pleasure or desire. Even those who had never previously met or heard of Amanda, were intrigued. And those who did remember her from before were, I felt sure, as astounded as I was by her almost unbelievable transformation. Sensing the intense fascination, she then began to talk about the Bible with one or two direct references to her own life experiences.

Amanda went on to say that her father and mother didn't give her the best start in life but when her father and her mother forsook her, then the Lord took her up, she was paraphrasing Psalms 27 verse 10. I was in total awe of Amanda that night; I was blown away by her wisdom and by her knowledge of the bible, wow I kept repeating to myself, "wow".

As the remarkable evening came to an end, I began to relax. I realized that Amanda was not going to say anything that might embarrass me; that was not her purpose. But why had she come to my Bible class tonight, rather than any other gathering? I knew part of the answer, she wanted not only to see me, but for me to see and know her in this new light, with her true soul, the one I had known and loved. Restored. I was pleased and proud about this. Yet at the same time I wanted to know more. What had she been doing in those years away in the wilderness? How had she managed to overcome her demons and turn her life around like this? Along with this curiosity I also realized, with a mixture of fear, guilt and excitement, that now she had come back—I did not want to let her go!

23

Confession

Amanda left the Bible class at the same time as the others. After the door had closed and I had wandered up to bed in something of a daze, I realized that I had no idea how to contact her. Maybe she would drop in unannounced again. If so, when? Perhaps she was waiting for me to make the next move, but in what way and would it be wise for me to do so?

The following day and unable to let it go, I rang Sister Bernice about some church matters and in the course of conversation, thanked her for inviting Amanda. As I had hoped, she then volunteered some information. Amanda was attending an inner-city church and had settled back into her hostel and was doing some volunteering. I asked, "do you, by any chance, have a number I could use to reach her as I'd like her to come along to our church one day, if possible." The smile on Sister Bernice's face told me she was happy to oblige.

Amanda and I were soon talking on the phone as if the lost years had never happened. We were two happy innocent school kids again. Best friends, laughing all the while and in a shy unspoken way, it felt like we were in love again. It seemed so natural to ask her over to my house. When she arrived, again it was just like good mates who didn't need to spell anything out but were simply easy in each other's company.

We sat and had a cup of coffee at the kitchen table just like we used to and began to reminisce about the old days at school; swapping anecdotes, joking and teasing one another. She always could out-talk me and dominated the conversation. But unlike the bad, God-hating days, there was no trace of resentment or hostility in her rapid-fire speech; just excitement and joy. She had, however, acquired a new habit, whenever I got the chance to speak, she leaned towards me as if not wanting to miss a single word I said. When I pointed this out, she said very eloquently, "some people listen with their lips and not with their ears. They have a reply for you without having heard all of what you had to say, some people hear you, without ever really listening."

I was struck by how true this was, how profound even, the very young Amanda, the green-eyed girl with the grown-up manner I had met on the steps, would not have said this, and truth be told, neither would the arrogant "Mandy" of later years, I wanted to find out more. "Tell me about your journey," I said. "Tell me how you went from Amanda to Mandy, and now you're Amanda again, but even more so, like a fuller, better, purer version. It must have been a long and difficult journey but only tell me if you can; if you want to."

There was a long pause as Amanda gazed into her coffee cup. Then, looking at me with her devastatingly beautiful green eyes she whispered, "Jason, you know that I love you don't you."

I immediately began to blush, "please, don't say that."

She repeated her words and did so several times more that evening was over, she said it in a smiling, teasing sort of way. Was she playing with my emotions, I didn't get that impression. There was a special kind of sincerity about her now, an openness that prompted her to speak exactly as she felt, without filtering or lying. It was all a part of her newfound self, she loved me, OK and I loved her. We were soul mates, I couldn't deny it, but what came next?

When it was time for her to leave, she gave me a peck on the cheek, and we said our fond farewells. I sat down and thought hard, during our cheerful light-hearted banter, it had been easy to ignore several elephants in the room. The elephant Amanda had so far ignored, was the lost years of her life and I had to admit that my interest was a lot more than that of a well-meaning Christian, whose Bible class she had recently attended. However, I would hear her story sooner than I expected.

Later, that same evening, at 10.30pm to be precise, my phone rang. There was no beating about the bush this time, on the contrary her forthrightness took my breath away.

"Jason, it took me a long time to learn how to like myself, let alone love myself."

"Why?" I asked.

Amanda said, "my past kept coming back to haunt me, the Bible says that God uses the foolish things of this world to confound the wise and that the foolishness of God is wiser than the wisdom of men. The weakness of God is stronger than the strength of men. Well, God used the foolish things of this world to put me back together again; he used a mirror to teach me to love myself."

"A mirror?" I said, not understanding the analogy.

"Yes Jason, a mirror, but I'll come to that later."

"So where does your story begin?" I asked.

"I guess it begins with my dad, you knew about him walking out on my mum and me."

"Yeah, yeah, that must have been tough," I said.

Amanda said, "it was roughly about the same time that we got together."

I said, "yes, I remember."

Then she said, "and then you went to Spain, and everything went wrong."

"Gareth came along you mean." Just saying the name made me feel sick.

"I'm not making excuses for myself and I'm not blaming him," she said.

"Why not?" I asked.

"You're going to hate me for saying this Jason, but I went with him willingly. OK, he had some sort of power over me. He manipulated me, but I could have said no, and you have to remember I was only a child at the time."

Feeling sorry for her I said, "he exploited your vulnerability."

"Yes, yes he did, I agree with you."

I then said, "so, he is to blame."

"Yes, I suppose so, but you're also being too generous to me by saying that. You were only away in Spain a matter of weeks, and as soon as your back was turned, I cheated on you, and in the worst way possible. And then when you came back, I felt so awful. It was like everything was ruined and it was my fault and I knew that if I told you I'd been with Gareth you'd never want to see me again."

"That's not true," I said quickly.

Amanda, retorted, "isn't it?"

"Well…" I couldn't reply, I didn't know whether it was true or not. The events we were talking about seemed like yesterday, but at the same time, so long ago. What would my reaction have been if she had confessed to me about Gareth straight away? I would have said that I forgave her but how sincere would that forgiveness have been?

A lump rose in my throat and I said, "I would have forgiven you."

"No, I had spoiled our love, I sort of turned in on myself and to Gareth. I can't deny that a part of me had wanted him anyway; for who he was."

I responded, "what?"

Amanda said, "OK, for who I thought he was."

I felt a painful stab of jealousy and said, "which was what?"

"Someone exciting, someone I wanted to give myself to. Someone who would treat me like a princess, like my dad did at one time."

The jealousy still searing in me, I indignantly said, "but didn't I treat you well?"

"Yes, of course you did but it wasn't the same, to me, Gareth was a man. A man who had strength, while you were still a boy, a really nice, harmless little boy."

"Good guys come last eh?" I was hurting I had to admit.

"I was wrong," said Amanda.

"OK!" I said.

"Gareth was weak, though he seemed strong, you were always the one with the real strength and the wisdom that I mistakenly thought he had. I was wrong there too and most importantly you had faith—a faith I deliberately threw away and mocked; because I loathed myself for what my own weakness had destroyed, which was our love."

I could feel tears welling in my eyes now, "Oh Amanda…"

"You don't know how many times I've wanted to turn the clock back, I hated myself for what happened."

I said, "you mustn't, you really mustn't."

"Oh Jason, I loved you so much, and I still do."

24

▪ Amanda Tells Her Story

The turmoil and confusion this latest expression of love threw me into, was immense, how had we come to this? More to the point, how had Amanda come to it? There was so much I didn't know or understand, and I felt as if I was being tugged in a dozen different directions. The following day we met up in a café and in a quiet corner, she began calmly and in her own time and words, telling me her whole story.

"You know Jason, my life really began when I was about four years old. What I mean is that it's my earliest memory and it still makes me smile with joy when I think of it. It was a Saturday afternoon, my mum had just returned from shopping and started to cook, my dad was in the garden clearing weeds and tidying up, he was quite a keen gardener. I was playing dress-up in my room and I could hear the lawnmower chugging away at the grass and I smelled the sweet fragrance of my mother's cooking.

The aroma of fried plantain, one of my favourite foods filled the house, every time I smell fried plantain it brings back that moment, like it's been captured in a bottle. The chugs of the lawnmower, the summer day, my mum and dad loving and contented, the memory of a perfect time when everyone was happy and at peace."

"You've told me some of this before," I said, "but never in as much detail, I can picture it, hey, I can even smell the fried plantain!"

Amanda smiled, "yes and you know what? It makes me happy to think about it, to take myself back to that scene; that very time and place."

I said, "because it was a safe place?"

Amanda continued, "yes, and it exists, it lives on for me and reminds me that there can be happiness in the world, and I had the gift of happiness, once."

At this last word she cast her eyes down and a shadow seemed to pass over her face. Then rallying herself, she went on. "I remember my dad's smile, I can see it now when I close my eyes. Such a kind, warm smile, full of absolute love and care. He would come into the room when I was dressing up as that princess and tell me I was going to marry a prince one day. And you know what? I believed him." She gazed at me directly as she said this and now it was my turn to look away.

I said, "that prince wasn't to be me though?"

Amanda paused a moment and sighed heavily, "I wish it could have been, you don't know how much, maybe now, if we gave it time, who knows."

"I'm sorry, I just can't think about that possibility," I said, "or rather I can, but I feel we ought not to."

Amanda said, "OK, OK, I won't bring it up again," there was an awkward silence for a while but, with no small effort, she continued, "oh, I just felt so lost when my dad went away, lost and then angry I think."

"I know," I said quietly.

Amanda said, "but I didn't tell you the worst bit."

I said, "which was?"

Then Amanda said, "that came later, when I found out he was getting married again and that he had a new princess on the way too."

"You mean…" I said.

She nodded, "yes, a daughter with his new partner. I never had siblings, no other child to share him with before. I had my dad all to myself, and then there was nothing, no part of him that was mine. He was gone with his new wife and his new princess and he didn't want to know me anymore. I know this sounds like I'm feeling sorry for myself, but he hurt me Jason, he hurt me really badly."

I responded, "sure, I know, I know."

"So, I sort of went off the rails and Gareth was there when I did."

I felt the familiar knot in my stomach at the mention of his name. As if reading my thoughts, she quickly added, "I know you were there for me too, but I've already explained to you why I chose him."

I said, "that's all right, but, if you don't mind my asking, I know it must be painful to talk about, you told me you were pregnant at fifteen, was it true?"

Amanda's face clouded over again, "do you really want to know? Yes, I was pregnant."

"What happened?" I asked.

"Gareth kept telling me to get rid of it and when I wouldn't, he attacked me."

The knot in my stomach grew tighter, "I thought it was something like that."

"It wasn't just a bit of pushing or shoving though, I'm talking about punching and kicking me repeatedly over days and weeks, and then…" she broke off and hid her face in her hands, which were shaking.

"Stop," I pleaded, "don't torture yourself with this."

"No, no, I need to tell you Jason, it's hard yes, and some of it might also sound like self-pity, like I'm wallowing in it all. I'm sorry to drop it all on you like this, to burden you."

"Don't say that, you're the one that has suffered; the burden is yours.

What does the Lord say about all ye who are heavy laden? You must talk about it, Amanda don't be afraid of my reaction, that's for me to deal with."

"Well, Gareth didn't want the baby he already seemed so jealous because I was giving it more attention than him, even though it wasn't yet born. Then one day I came home and found him with another woman."

"Oh, you mean they were…? I asked

"Yeah, it was pretty obvious they were in bed together, when I entered the room, the woman ran out and left the house. I went downstairs shaking and when Gareth followed me, I flew into a rage, screaming at him. Without thinking he picked up a kitchen knife and lunged at me. It caught me in my shoulder, and then in my left hand as I lifted my hand to protect myself. I was told by the doctors the knife wound just missed an artery and I was lucky to be alive, I went into depression for weeks after that."

I could not help recoiling in sheer disgust and horror, Amanda sat very still now. Her hands had stopped shaking, tears rolled down her face. With it was the sense of some heavy load falling from her, leaving behind a quiet, thoughtful kind of sadness. "That's what caused the miscarriage," she said very softly. That was when we were in Manchester, he forced me to lie to the police and say that I was mugged at knifepoint to stop him from going to jail.

Afterwards Gareth used to disappear for long periods of time, I was on my own a lot. I felt awful, but I covered it up, or at least tried to."

My attempt to console her I said, "you were suffering from rejection, depression and on top of it all, physical and mental abuse, and you felt you had no one to turn to." I couldn't help myself, my heart was breaking for Amanda and what she had been through, I wanted desperately to help her get past it all.

"You could say that," she smiled warmly knowing what I was trying to do. "But I just couldn't see it at the time, I was lost and hopeless and it all turned to resentment."

I said, "I wish I had been more understanding and more capable, I should have tried to help you."

Amanda, reached out and pressed my hand, "you did, you did, but you were so young. We both were, it's hard to see what's happening sometimes; to ourselves and to others. Perhaps especially when we're close to them, I rejected your help if you remember?"

I closed my eyes for a moment, praying for the strength to listen, not to let my own feelings crowd in on what Amanda was telling me. I could feel how extremely hard it was for her. "Go on," I said, "tell me what happened in Manchester, after you lost the baby, but only if you want to."

Amanda responded, "I do, I do…well…I was taken into the hospital and I was there for a while."

"How long?" I asked.

Amanda then said, "I don't remember exactly, it just seemed like a very long time, then I came back to London with Gareth." I said, "that's when I saw you that day, outside the shop, you looked so unwell."

"I was I suppose, well anyway, we then went back to Manchester but again, I was alone a lot of the time," Amanda said.

I asked, "where was Gareth?"

Amanda said, "out on business."

I quickly added, "dealing drugs, you mean."

Amanda nodded.

I said, "oh Amanda, I'm so sorry."

Amanda asked, "what for, it wasn't your fault, none of it was your fault."

"I should have gone to the police long before that, the night I came to your house and Gareth hit me, I knew he was beating you up. I could see the bruises, but I was a coward!" I buried my head in my hands.

"No, you mustn't blame yourself, you must have felt that reporting him could have made things worse for me, she said.

"If that was so, then I made the wrong decision," I said.

Amanda sighed and tilted her head from side to side as if trying to weigh this up. "Perhaps, perhaps not," she said. "But there's something else you have to take into account. Gareth is a very smooth operator and a very good actor, who can change roles in the blink of an eye. One minute he'd be hitting me and the next, telling me how much he cared about me and loved me; especially in front of other people."

I added, "you mean he put on a front!"

Amanda agreed with me and said, "exactly; he even had me fooled with his apologies and his gentlemanly act. I'm sure those that didn't know him would have been taken in by it."

I said, "but what about the police? I mean he has a criminal record, right?"

"That's true, but I guess I was still scared of him too, and as I said, he could switch to "Mr Nice Guy" in a flash, I'm ashamed to say that I fell for it more than once, I also thought I might change him if I stuck by him."

"Stand by your man, eh?" I said.

Amanda shrugged, "I was naïve, what can I say? Naïve and afraid."

"No one is blaming you," I hastened to add, "you know, after you left when your mum moved out, I used to walk past your house quite a lot. It was boarded up and every time I went by, I was hoping I would find it like it used to be when we first met. I was stupid, a childish dreamer, no wonder you soon tired of me! I should have tried to find you at least."

Amanda spread out her hands, "where would you have looked? I changed my phone number, we were living in a squat in Manchester, there was nothing you could have done."

"I did pray, but obviously not hard enough," I said dejectedly.

Amanda held my gaze, "Jason, "she said quietly, "you might be wrong there."

25

Deliverance

"Shall we have another coffee?" I said.

"I think we'd better," smiled Amanda, "this café will go bust if we just sit here talking all day! I'll get them this time."

We ordered more coffee and Amanda continued her story.

"After losing the baby I became really depressed. Then one night, whilst looking in the mirror, I heard the sound of bells ringing. I had just finished smoking some weed and thought I was going crazy. I went out of the house, sat in a pub and got totally drunk, a guy took me back to his place and…"

"You don't have to go on," I told her, I could see how painful retelling the story was becoming.

"Yes, I'm sorry Jason but if you can bear with me, I have to continue."

"Only if you want to Amanda, only if you want to."

"Well, he raped me, but it wasn't just him. There were other men there too and they all did it, one after another. They forced themselves upon me, I was helpless. Afterwards they beat me up and threatened me saying that if ever I told anyone, they would hunt me down and kill me. The next day I hated myself even more than ever, I was suicidal and wanted out of there. Gareth was nowhere to be found, he had other girlfriends and made no attempt to hide the fact. I had no one to help me, so, I turned to drink and weed to numb the pain."

Listening to Amanda whilst watching her cry, was becoming too much for me. My eyes flooded with tears; I could barely see her through them. I decided that we needed to go somewhere private, as we were drawing attention to ourselves. Gently holding her by the hand, I walked her out of the Café and walked towards the park. As we walked, unaware of our surroundings Amanda continued to tell her story.

"I've done a lot of soul-searching over the last year and have had to confront some unpleasant truths about myself and about some of the things I've done and been involved in. It wasn't just Gareth doing the crime, I was colluding with him. We were renting an apartment in Manchester and selling drugs to people in the area. We knew that some of the women we supplied couldn't pay for them. So, we used our place as a brothel, prostituted the girls and made a lot of cash doing it. There was one occasion when I came back to London and you saw me battered and bruised, that was after one of our suppliers turned on us and nearly killed us both."

"Oh Amanda, if only I had known about this…"

"But even that didn't put me off, the money was too easy for me. I was heavily involved with the drug culture, until I had become a victim of it. Oh Jason! I've seen people shot and stabbed but the most shaming part for me, was that it all felt meaningless. I had given myself up to quick highs and easy money, which had dehumanised me. I had lost any sense of empathy for people. I can say that now, though I burn with shame to admit it. And as for thinking I could change Gareth, I wasn't even trying, I was as bad as he was."

"That cannot be true," I protested.

"He carried on beating me up and I knew he didn't care about me one bit, and yes, I could have got out of it If I wanted to."

I asked, "then why didn't you."

"When you're in it, it takes you over—you lose control. What drove me to the edge was when he ended up selling me to the same supplier that nearly killed the two of us, because he owed him money."

"Selling you, what on earth do you mean," I asked.

Amanda continued, "to do whatever he wanted with me, rape me whenever he felt like it. Use me as his punch bag whenever he wanted, and to take out his aggression on me if he wanted."

There were tears of anger and pity in my eyes, "oh Amanda, I don't know what to say, I'm so very, very sorry."

Amanda said, "he was a real gangster, too…made Gareth look like a beginner, anyway, it was the same story as with Gareth really, only even more brutal, if that's possible."

I stared at her, still struggling for words, "how… I mean, how did it end?"

"There seemed to be only one way I could escape him and that was through violence. So, I took a knife from the kitchen drawer one day and stabbed him. Then I ran out of his house and never stopped running. I wasn't sure if I killed him or not, but a few months later I saw him driving down the road. He looked at me after shaping his fingers like a gun and pointed them at me as if to pull the trigger. I didn't know whether to feel relieved or scared. Scared at the thought he would kill me or relieved that after death there would be no more pain."

"Woah, Amanda! So, you were completely on your own after getting away from this other guy?"

"Yes, I tried to find Gareth, but he seemed to have disappeared. I couldn't focus on anything, I couldn't function. Getting a job or studying or having any sort of normal life ever again seemed impossible. My dad was gone, I had lost touch with my mum and had no friends or relatives I could turn to. It was as if my life had come to an end. I began to hear voices in my head."

"Voices? Whose voices? What were they saying?" I asked.

"All sorts of different voices but no-one I knew, they were all telling me the same thing. That my life was pointless. That there was no hope, no future and I was a waste of space. They were telling me there was only one last act my miserable soul could perform in this cruel ugly world, which no longer wanted me. The one thing left in my power, so, I decided to do it, I decided to kill myself."

"NO!" I said.

"Why not? My existence was not only pointless, but I was in torment. I had tried drugs and money and drink, but nothing had taken the pain away, there was only one option left."

In a hushed voice, I said, "so what did you do?"

"It was so easy, I just took some pills, lots of them, and downed them with a bottle of whiskey. I ended up in the hospital having my stomach pumped."

I asked, "how did you get to the hospital?"

"To this day, I don't know, I was shacked up in a bedsit and would entertain men so that I could eat and pay my bills. Perhaps one of them found me and called an ambulance. To this day, I'm surprised that I am still alive."

"Thank God," I said.

"Yes, thank God indeed," Amanda said, looking at me now with a clear, purposeful look in her eyes.

"Then one day I just got on a train back to London, it was several years after I had first left home. I suppose I was trying to go back in every sense of the word."

I said, "to the smell of fried plantain and the sound of the lawnmower in the garden?"

Amanda replied, "yes, but I was looking for something that wasn't there anymore."

I hesitated before saying, "I was here."

"Yes, you were, and I think that was the one thing that really kept me going, it gave me the will to live again, knowing you were alive in the world."

"Why didn't you come and find me straightaway?"

"I wasn't worthy of you, I had to change first, change properly and wholly; you know what I mean?"

I nodded, I truly knew what she meant.

"I didn't know it though, not yet, I still really didn't have a clue what I was doing, or where I was going. I needed somewhere to stay in London and found a very hostile and unfriendly bedsit that I rented and again not having any money I used what I had, to make some. I became friends with one of the girls who lived in another bedsit in the same building and it turned out that she had become a Christian. She badgered me to go to church, but in my head, God couldn't love someone as wretched as me. After all I had done, how could He possibly want me to turn to Him. But one day she invited me along to church and I made the sad mistake of going. I wasn't expecting what took place that night, I apprehensively walked into the church and when I did, I just couldn't stop crying, so much so, it became very embarrassing. The pastor brought a very strong presence into the room, as if someone else was with her. I kept thinking, she's brought her guardian angel with her. In fact, there was another person with her and do you know who it was…it was Sister Bernice. The pastor quoted a verse from the Bible that night that literally changed my life, it was Psalm 139, verse 14:

I praise you, for I am fearfully and wonderfully made. Wonderful are your works; my soul knows it very well. As soon as I heard these words something very remarkable happened to me."

"Can you describe it?" I asked.

"Well, it wasn't pleasant, I began screaming, there and then in the room. I became uncontrollable I didn't know what was happening to me, I couldn't help myself. I was told later that it took Sister Bernice, who as you know isn't small, and five other ladies to hold me down. It was pandemonium! Other people were screaming, too, scared by what seemed like me having a fit but something much more alarming, more profound was happening. It was like nothing they had ever witnessed before, it was certainly like nothing I had ever felt or experienced. I later discovered that I had gone through what was called "deliverance." It was terrible, terrible, but extraordinary too. Afterwards, like a sudden intense fever leaving me, I felt so different."

"In what way?" I said.

"Better, but not just better, completely changed. Light and free as though a great weight had been lifted from me. That Sunday my friend invited me to church, I followed her, not knowing it was your church that she was taking me to. I was greeted by one of the loveliest women I had ever met, Mother Rachel they called her. She made me feel so welcomed and wanted, I will never forget that moment. The service went well, and I loved the Praise and Worship, I couldn't understand the preacher though, he was quoting so much scripture, which made no sense to me at the time. What did make a deep impression on me was the banner that read, "The Spirit of the Lord Is in This Place."

I had Goosebumps all throughout the service and I couldn't stop crying. Someone came over to me and said it was the Holy Spirit embracing me, but I still didn't understand. The preacher finished his message and called for sinners to repent and to give their lives to Christ. At the time I knew I was a sinner but didn't know what to do about it. Despite the deliverance, a part of me still didn't quite get what was happening. Then one of the other ministers asked if I would like to be prayed for.

I sat still for several minutes, but then I got up and walked to the altar with him, that's when I saw you."

"I didn't see you, I'm sorry," I said.

Amanda expressed, "it was a shock for me seeing you there, I couldn't face you, not yet."

I said, "Amanda, you're telling me the story, like someone who has never been to Church before, you were more devout than me."

Amanda responded, "I know Jason, but years in the wilderness seemed to have erased all of what I knew, the drink and the drugs seemed to have stolen the seed that was planted all those years ago."

I said, "anyway, Sister Bernice did mention that you went missing for a while but several weeks later, you came to the Bible class at my house."

Amanda said, "yes, Sister Bernice suggested it, I think she knew more than she let on. Well, that's the story, the story of how I was lost, but now am found. Yes, I am found and I believe I have you to thank. You drew me to the fold, to Salvation. Drew me invisibly, almost unknowingly through your faith and through your continued prayers for me."

"I cannot claim any credit, Amanda," I said truly humbled by all I was hearing, "this is the Lord's work, I am simply glad, actually, glad isn't the right word, I'm overjoyed and amazed! My heart and soul give thanks, no words can truly do justice to how I feel after hearing your journey and now, here you are," I said.

"Here we are," Amanda said.

I gazed into her beautiful green eyes; the windows of the soul. A soul newly born and at peace, but what of my peace, I wondered? How could I begin to calm the torrent of emotions now coursing through me?

26

Dangerous Desire

Amanda was right, here we were, our present lives were as closely intertwined as ever but although we could not change the past, the present could not be ignored either. Amanda had found if not happiness, at least the path towards it through faith. Yet she remained fragile and had come to me for a reason. Was it just a matter of friendship, or was she hoping for something more? She had grown into a very attractive young woman, who seemed interested in me now, and I could not deny the temptation to touch and hold and kiss her. I had to remain strong and resist the temptation. I'd seen too many men and women of the cloth, fall from grace. For both moral reasons and for self-preservation, I had to try to resist.

Amanda had been through a terrible time, she was still unstable and needed the reassurance of a friend whom she could trust, not an affair with a former childhood sweetheart to prop up her self-esteem. I had to avoid leading her on and at the same time, not hurt her by an outright rejection. My task was simply to be there for her, but it was not going to be easy. Because at the same time, another thought continued to haunt me. Supposing Amanda was my true love and we were meant for each other after all? If that were the case, I wouldn't be exploiting her but doing the right thing, wouldn't I?

I sat up late into the night thinking it all over, but just couldn't find an answer. When I finally went to bed exhausted, all I could see were Amanda's beautiful green eyes staring into mine, with a look of wonder and innocence and devotion. Was she the devil in disguise, come to tempt me, or the light of my life; the light I was now being asked to follow?

I awoke with a burning desire to see Amanda again immediately. Perhaps it was just as well that I had to go to work that day to take my mind off her. But on returning home that evening, I felt my heart leap with pleasure on seeing her number flash up when my phone rang.

"Hi Jason," she said.

"Hi! How are you doing?" was my reply.

"Good, good, I just wondered if we could carry on with our discussion," she said.

"Sure," I said.

Then Amanda said, "or rather, if I carried on talking about myself while you listened!"

"That's what I'm here for, well, you know what I mean."

"You are wonderful," Amanda said.

I said, "I don't think so, really."

"Yes, you are… I mean it, you're so caring and selfless; you always were. It's just that I never saw it until now, it's one of the reasons I love you," she said.

I paused a split second before replying awkwardly, "don't say that, please."

Then Amanda said, "Why? There's not enough love in the world, didn't you always used to say that?"

"I… can't remember," was my response.

"And what's wrong with loving you? I know you love me too," she said.

This time I paused even longer before saying quietly, "Amanda, you broke my heart, what's to say it won't happen again?"

Now it was her turn to go silent, "I know," she then said flatly, "Jason, I care too much about you to put you through that again."

I could feel my voice shaking now, "of course, I do love you Amanda and I always have. We're special to each other; we both know that, but…"

Amanda interrupted, "but not in that way, we love each other but we can't be lovers, is that what you're saying?"

"No! Yes! I mean… I don't know, it's just that…" I could feel myself going hot with shame, guilt, confusion, embarrassment and desire all at once. I wanted to be with Amanda so much at that moment that I was aching with desire to hold her close, kiss her beautiful lips and take her to bed…oh God!

"Jason just in case I forget, one of the reasons why I went missing after meeting Sister Bernice was because when I was still living in the bedsit, I was introduced to someone who was believed to be a very good person and he became my prayer partner. We prayed together regularly, he was always so kind and considerate and had so much knowledge of the Bible. I felt reassured and comforted by him. Then one night when we were alone, he tried to seduce me. it was a great shock to me that someone could seem so good, so holy, and… you know. I know all about pretentiousness, and false piety, and I know you're not like that."

I said, "yes, yes of course, the devil can be subtle, I'm sorry that happened to you, he took terrible advantage of your trust."

Amanda said, "it was another lesson, a good lesson, and I think it taught me to recognise true goodness."

I said, "good, yes."

"The goodness of someone like you Jason," Amanda said.

"No," I said.

"What hurt me most is that the gentleman attends your church and sits there as though it never happened. There must be something about me that attracts the wrong kind of guy. Jason, I know you're trying to protect yourself and I must accept that, but it doesn't stop me feeling the way I do about you and it never will."

"Oh Amanda!" I said.

Amanda responded, "what?"

"Listen, I... I must see you," I said.

"Oh, sure, when?" Amanda said.

I said, "tonight, now."

Amanda responded, "come to my flat."

Half an hour later Amanda and I were in her flat, the curtains were closed, and I was kissing her passionately.

27

■ Passion and Destiny

What happened next was that Amanda and I went to bed, being inexperienced, I had always thought that when the right moment happened, I would be completely inadequate. My worries were groundless. Amanda's sheer physical beauty, her aroma, her soft sweet lips and the touch of her skin next to mine, took my body by storm. Undressing I felt no embarrassment, only desire.

We did not rush, it was as if we were dancing. The slow, silent, rhythmic music of our bodies was infinitely graceful and set the tempo of this dance. I had never dreamed that lovemaking could be so tender or so perfect, afterwards we slept like children, enfolded in each other's arms.

My eyes opened up to a sunlit room, we had forgotten to close the curtains. Amanda was already up, and I could smell the aroma of fresh coffee. The silly grin on my face felt suddenly rigid, as if it were painted on, what had I done? Guilt, like a thunderbolt, shot through me. At that moment Amanda appeared in the doorway bearing two mugs. She was wearing a pretty silk dressing gown, her hair loose. She looked stunning! For a moment, she stood looking at me, her smile part mischievous and part indulgent, playing on her lips; taking me in as if for the first time, like a prized new possession.

She brought the coffee over and sat beside me on the bed and said, "here."

I said, "thanks."

Amanda asked, "how are you?"

I breathed out and "OK, you?"

She laughed and then nodded, "OK, yeah; no, that's a lie. I'm actually over the moon, walking on air, dancing with the angels; all that and more my love." She threw back her head and laughed, it was the most beautiful sound I had ever heard.

I said, "listen, we need to have a talk."

Amanda said, "oh, we're going to have lots of talks Jason, for the rest of our lives."

I said, "you mean, you don't think this was just a…"

"I love you Jason, I told you I did and as conceited as this may sound, I think, no I know, that you love me too."

I sat up, squinting in the sunlight and ran my hand through my hair. My thoughts were tumbling against one another and the thudding guilt was continually overwhelming all of them. I said, "I don't want to be hurt again."

Amanda nodded, she looked at me, gravely now, "I don't want to force you into anything, but what we did last night happened and it was the best thing ever for me. If you say you want to walk away from me now, I swear on the Bible I will respect that. I'll be sad, but I'll respect it. And don't think I'll go to pieces or hurt myself because of it. I'm past all that now. God took me past it a long time ago, I'm responsible for my own actions, so there'll be no emotional blackmail, no need to pity me or feel obliged." She spoke so calmly; serious yet in control.

I sighed, a great big sigh, as if I had arrived in paradise. But a voice in my head was already telling me I had a return ticket and I had to use it or else. Another voice was whispering;

Don't be a fool. Stay. Stay. This is real, this is where you belong. Don't throw it all away now you've come this far. The world of yesterday is the illusion, and this is the reality. Your dream has become reality, take it; Amanda knew.

"Tell me something, honestly Jason, do you really love me?"

I swallowed hard, even thinking about this felt difficult. "It's a difficult question," I was desperately trying to guard my heart, "love is difficult, but if you've any doubts about me, then it's best to do nothing right now. But I don't think you want to do nothing, I think we both know what's happened."

Amanda reached out and took my hand in hers. She looked deep into my eyes and in a voice so intense it was almost hypnotic, said, "I believe that what happened between us last night was meant to be Jason. It was meant to be, ever since we were children. Everything that's happened in between has been some sort of test and it's all been leading up to this moment." Leaning towards me she kissed me softly on the lips. The next moment we were making love again, as naturally and blissfully as we had done just a few hours before.

As we lay back together on the pillows, Amanda murmured, "you do realize this is not just physical Jason. Don't get me wrong, physical is nice." She gave a sweet, gurgling laugh. "Physical is good, very good, you know what I'm saying, but you and I have always been soul mates." Then she laid her head against my chest and rubbed it slowly and sensually, "this is the icing on the cake."

"If we eat too much of it, we might get sick," I said, Amanda responded with her gurgling laugh again, how I loved that.

"Don't worry my dear," she said, nuzzling my ear, "we are going to have lots of nutritious fillings too!"

"Slow down," I said nervously, "we don't want to jump the gun."

She sat up and leaned on her elbow, looking down at me, "who's jumping? We've known each other most of our lives. More like you've loved me all your life. You carried on caring about me when no one else did. For years you were the only one who could see the mistakes I was making, the hurt I was feeling inside. That means something, something important, something that can't be ignored. People might think me wrong to say this, but I think God brought me back for you Jason. And now God has brought us together, there is no going back." As she spoke, I knew she was right, there was no going back, I wanted to tell the world. From adolescence to adulthood I had kept myself and vowed to myself that I would remain a virgin until the day that I would give myself to my wife; on that night I broke my vow and a part of me felt guilty for doing so.

28

∎Feeling Guilty

The more I thought about making a clean breast of things, the more afraid, shameful and miserable I felt. Two days had passed, and I had still not decided on when or how, I was going to do it. Once done, it would be an irrevocable step; words spoken cannot be unspoken. Just like a letter, a text or an email once delivered, cannot be unsent. The world changes with our every action, but I asked myself, hadn't it already changed on the night that Amanda and I made love? I knew I had committed a grievous crime against God and now I had to tell my Pastor. But I couldn't, and if I tried to pretend nothing had happened my life would be impossible. True, I could say nothing, and he might never be any the wiser. I felt certain that Amanda would let things be and not cause any kind of trouble in that direction. The only loose tongue would be mine and my conscience would dictate that sooner or later I would have to confess. That was not, however, the scenario I was envisaging. My life was now where it was. I wanted to be with Amanda forever, no question. If I was honest, she had been right, I had loved her from the very beginning, right from the first time we met as children.

My sole angst now, was about doing the right thing; about speaking to a friend, my pastor, who had such high regard for me. I felt as though I had let him down and betrayed his trust. And what about my mother? There would be no mercy from her; she'd be livid! She was too good a person, I never wanted to hurt her, and the thought only made it worse. Inside, my mother had always told me to keep myself until the day of my marriage. What can I tell her now? What can I say to my pastor?

Amanda seemed to know immediately how I was feeling and kept telling me it was meant to be. I didn't even have to say anything she just looked at my face and nodded calmly. Not for the first time, I got the impression she was telepathic, that she had some kind of sixth sense. As we sat over dinner that evening, I could feel her relax more, as if the last of her burdens had fallen from her shoulders. We belonged to each other now—physically, mentally and spiritually. I felt so happy I just wanted to laugh and tell people all day long, how happy I was. Everyone was my friend. From the man in the shop to the passengers on the train to my boss and work colleagues, to the homeless guy on the street that I met on my way home from work. The look on his face when I gave him five pounds was quite a sight to see.

I stayed at Amanda's flat, that night; she was adamant about it. She was busily spring-cleaning and rearranging everything to make me feel at home, as if I belonged there; even though I had my own flat. As I made myself comfortable, I started to think about what our permanent living arrangements might be like. There was so much to do and talk about, but we were in no hurry. The only thing that seemed to matter was us being together.

On the weekend we went out and I bought flowers, magazines, DVDs; an expensive coffee machine and clothes for both of us. Amanda was disapproving and tried to stop me behaving so wildly with my money. But she could see it was making me happy and that I wouldn't hold back. Seeing the homeless guy again, I gave him ten pounds, this time. Amanda, for some reason, apologised to him. I think he thought we were both crazy, perhaps we were, later that evening, we talked about marriage.

As the weeks went by, Amanda and I settled into a routine. We had already started to resemble an old married couple and the feeling of guilt had long since passed. We were getting married, so what was the problem?

We would leave the flat at the same time each morning, kiss briefly, she would then head off to the bus stop to go to work; while I walked in the opposite direction to get to the railway station. In the evenings, she was usually home first and there would always be a tantalising aroma coming from the kitchen when I got back. On the weekends, I would insist on cooking, trying hard to match her culinary skills. I had bought a raft of books by the top TV chefs; making her laugh as I studied the recipes as if they were a Bible text. Which brings me to the elephant in the room. Since that first earth shattering night, neither of us had been to church or been in touch with our fellowship. I had, however, phoned my mum several times and made plans to meet her in town for lunch. We met up at quite a plush restaurant, she was looking well, and I told her so.

"Thank you," she replied, "I feel well, I am blessed and how are you son?"

"Good, good," I looked down.

"No need to be bashful," mum said.

"I'm not, honestly, I'm not," funny how your mother can make you squirm, whatever your age.

"Why don't you bring Amanda around?" she asked.

I replied, "I will, soon."

Then mum said, "and it'll be nice to see you both in church."

I said, "yes, we must come, how's Richard?"

This time my mother hesitated, but only for a second, "oh, yes he's good too, I do wish you'd call him one day."

I asked, "he's not in any trouble, is he?"

My mum beamed, "no, no dear, quite the opposite."

I quickly said, "oh, I'm glad."

Mum said, "hmm, he'll tell you all about it, I'm sure."

At that point I had to go, as I was due back at work.

Again, it had been rather cowardly of me, but I had avoided going to see my mum at home; just in case anyone from the church happened to be there. I didn't want any awkwardness; without saying as much, I think we both knew the time had come for us to go back to church and resume our worship, this time as a couple. But only when we felt the moment was right, then one day I got a surprise.

It was about three months after we had become serious about each other. We were in a department store on one of our Saturday shopping trips and Amanda had gone into a cubicle to try on some clothes. It was then I noticed my brother Richard, I had been meaning to get in touch with him, my mum's reminder had been playing on my conscience. I should have found the time to see my own brother before now; well, here he was. As I moved closer, I realized why perhaps my mum had smiled at the mention of his name, when normally she would have sighed and shaken her head. Richard was wearing smart casual clothes, and his wary, arrogant demeanour seemed to have disappeared. Instead he stood relaxed and serene, his arms folded and leaning against a pillar. I went over and laid a hand on his shoulder, "and what might you be doing in the women's-wear section?" I asked, laughing with the sheer pleasure of seeing my brother.

"Jason!" Richard jumped as if electrified.

"Sorry Rich, I didn't mean to startle you. You're looking really smart by the way."

"Oh, thanks, Yeah," he replied, the relaxed air had gone, and he shifted from one foot to the other, avoiding my eye. Why was he suddenly embarrassed? At that moment, a sales assistant came up to Richard and held out a garment. The bizarre thought suddenly popped into my head that my brother had become a cross dresser. How ought I to handle this I wondered?

"Oh sir," said the assistant, "could you tell the lady we've also found the dress in the next size down like she asked for. Would she like to try that as well?" She gestured towards the changing cubicles.

Ah, of course! Funny, I had never thought of Richard having a girlfriend, or at least not one he would go shopping with patiently on a Saturday. Well, this would be nice I thought. When Amanda appeared, the two of them could meet.

It was Richard's girlfriend who emerged from the cubicles first. "What do you think Richard? Oh!" She tailed off and stared at me, I stared back. Standing there in a shiny new dress with the labels still attached, was the girl that had once offered to be a witness to the altercation that I had with Gareth several years ago; when he had almost knocked me over. She was the girl that offered me the tissue, what a small world, surely, she would remember Amanda.

29

▪Love All

Shortly afterwards, Amanda came out of her cubicle. She took a few seconds to register the scene. "Oh! Hi! This is nice!" she exclaimed flashing a big smile at Richard and his girlfriend.

Rich mumbled, "hi, Mandy, you alright?"

I said, "I'm good, I'm good, yeah. What are you both doing here? Sorry, that was a stupid question, you're shopping obviously."

Rich gave me a strange look and said, "OK, OK, that's cool, so, erm, listen. I was just telling Jason, I have been seeing Holly for a few months now." Amanda's hand flew to her mouth, her eyes lighting up with excitement, "Oh my gosh! I knew it! I mean, as soon as I saw you both I thought there was something. But it's such a surprise, if you know what I mean. But hey, a lovely surprise, don't you think so Jason?"

I said, "yeah."

Amanda said almost dancing with joy, "we could make a foursome for dinner tonight!"

"Sure, why not," smiled Holly.

"Maybe not tonight. it's just that"...began Richard.

Amanda interjected and said, "oh sorry, short notice, I know. That's me all over, impulsive, isn't that right Jason? Oh, but who am I telling!" Amanda laughed and touched Richard's arm in a friendly gesture. She seemed genuinely thrilled by the whole turn of events. "But let's do it soon, oh, this couldn't have been better if we'd planned it! Just like one of those romantic comedies, isn't it!"

Richard seemed keen to leave, "OK Jason, take care of yourself yeah and you too Amanda."

"Sure," I said. "good to see you both."

Holly said, "hold on a minute, I know you, don't I? You're Amanda, you're the girl that went out with Gareth, who ended up punching Jason."

"Pipe down Holly, you're embarrassing me," squirmed Richard, "the two of them are an item now."

"How did you know Richard?" I asked.

Silence filled the area around where we were all standing, it was awkward. Then Amanda said, "Jason are you ready now, I've finished shopping and I'd like to go home now."

I said, "Richard, Holly it's been great seeing you both, we must catch-up one day."

Richard's response was, "Jason I'll call you." As we walked away, I could see the hurt on Amanda's face, so I gently took her by the hand and comforted her.

A we headed to the exit, Richard shouted, "Jason don't forget to go to church, it's where you belong and you Amanda!"

"Well, well!" Amanda said as we left the store and headed home.

I echoed, "well, well."

Amanda said, "it's so nice isn't it, that they're together, she'll keep Richard on the right path. No more getting into trouble. He looked so happy, embarrassed, but happy. You are pleased for your brother, aren't you?"

"Yes, yes of course, I am. It just takes a bit of getting used to that's all. Seeing the two of them together just now, and it doesn't look like a flash in the pan to me. They seemed well-suited, like they were made for each other, just like you and me sweetheart."

"I just don't want Rich to get hurt."

Amanda joined in and said, "of course, not, especially now he's turned the corner and no longer involved in crime, I bet he's even going to church too."

"I bet so, that's what my mum was on about."

"Your mum?" Amanda said.

I said, "I saw her in town recently, she hinted that something was happening with Richard, something good; but she was shy about telling me exactly what it was."

Then Amanda said, "well, now you know and it's a very good thing. Praise the Lord! And yes, your mum and Richard are right, it's time for you and me to go back to church. Everything has turned out for the best." She squeezed my arm lovingly and said, "come on, I'll treat you to a cappuccino!"

That night, I lay awake listening to Amanda's soft, rhythmic breathing as she slept. I thought over the events of the day, which seemed like a dream. Or as Amanda had rightly said, a scene from a romantic movie. There had been four people, two of whom had loved each other since childhood but through various trials, had never managed to get together. Then after many long years, they had stepped through the looking glass and made their dream come alive. To complete the circle of perfection, the hero's troubled brother had then found happiness and redemption with the faithful soul who had helped the hero in years past. Amanda was right, we had to thank God for this divine blessing, and it must be done in church.

The following day we began to discuss marriage.

As we drank coffee at the breakfast table, Amanda said, "Your mum will be so proud of you, proud and happy."

I smiled, "you know what would make me proud, apart from having you as my wife? A home of our own, this flat of yours is great, but just think for a minute, what if we had a house with a proper garden..."

Amanda asked, "could we afford it?"

I said, "we could if we sell my flat as well, and maybe move out of London."

Amanda questioned, "wouldn't your mum miss you?"

"Richard's close by, and his new young lady, I'm sure he will pop in on Mum from time to time, or perhaps we could all move to the country."

Amanda said, "be farmers? Ooh-argh!" Amanda stuck a spoon in her mouth.

I said, "grow stuff at any rate."

"Sounds great, maybe we should have a double wedding, and all share a huge house—your mum, me, you and Richard and Holly, I do hope he marries her." Amanda said.

"Yeah, me too, even though her memories of me aren't the best, I still think she's a nice person and I do like her. I will be very surprised if Holly changes Rich's mind about marriage. I never thought he'd get married, not in a million years!"

Amanda said, "well, there's a lot of things that have happened, which we'd never have predicted."

"True," I said.

Amanda said, "I like the idea of a big garden by the way."

"For growing things?" I asked.

Amanda, said, "yeah, but more importantly, it'd be great for the kids."

"Kids?" I said.

Amanda got up and took my hands, pulling them around her waist, and said "our kids, silly."

"I hadn't thought about that," I had a sudden spasm of alarm, mixed with excitement. "Kids?! "Amanda, you're not...?"

"No, no," she stroked my hair, "there are no more surprises, but..." before Amanda could finish her sentence, I rudely interrupted...

"Ah, I had never considered children, now suddenly I could picture it. You and me, a mother and father to one, two or maybe three, wonderful little people. Loving them without condition and watching them grow up. Wow, Me, a father. WOW!" Then I remembered: Amanda had almost been a mother once. Gently I said, "Erm, the thing is… sorry. Perhaps this isn't the time to bring this up, but would you be able to, after what happened with Gareth I mean?"

Amanda's head dropped as she gently whispered, "the doctor told me that I may never have children again. I have lived with the pain of not bearing a child for years and the pain of it still hurts to this day."

I kissed her cheek and told her I will love her until the day she dies, and if she desperately wanted a child, we would adopt one.

30

Wedding Plans

After initially laughing at my suggestion that we move to the country, Amanda seemed to warm to the idea. Real estate brochures from Norfolk, Sussex and, Kent began to arrive. After coming home from work, Amanda would sit cross-legged on the sofa, surfing the internet for houses, bungalows, barns, new builds, conversions; most of them in places I had barely heard of.

"I don't think we can afford a stately home," I said one evening, as she showed me photos of some enormous properties, with equally enormous price tags.

Amanda said, "I'm sure there'd be room to negotiate on the asking prices," Amanda could sound scarily business-like sometimes.

I said, "I think we'd better lower our sights to a more realistic level."

"You said you wanted a farm," she said.

"There's no way we'll ever be able to buy a farm," I said.

"You'd be surprised," replied Amanda, scrolling up and down a series of pictures with lots of green fields and naturally blue skies. "Especially if we sell both our flats and if we are prepared to look further out."

"Even then the Home Counties is definitely out—for a farm I mean, wouldn't a decent sized garden be enough?"

Amanda signed, "it would, but you know me."

I laughed, "do I…I sometimes wonder."

Amanda said, "oh Jason, I do love you, you're so… sensible."

I replied, "someone has to be."

Amanda said, "I'm a dreamer, I know it."

I said, "that's not how you seemed to me all those years ago."

Amanda quickly said, "when we were kids."

I said, "yeah, you seemed so together, older than your years. I felt like I was the one doing the dreaming. Dreaming that I could be your boyfriend, take you out, get married and live in a little house of our own."

Then Amanda said, "oh, speaking of which…" suddenly pushing her laptop aside, she took my hand excitedly in hers and said, "I've been looking at wedding venues, I know, we haven't discussed it, but we've got to start somewhere, so…"

Now it was my turn to interrupt, "hang on," I said, "when you say, "wedding venues," are we talking about a church?"

"For the actual ceremony, most definitely sweetheart!" Amanda looked at me earnestly and said, "and I'm assuming you'd prefer it to be your church, our church, yes?"

I nodded, "yes, I think my mum would be upset if I didn't, if you put it that way."

Then Amanda said, "ok, now for the reception I think I've found the perfect place and they could fit us in next summer."

I said, "where?"

Amanda quickly said, "a really lovely country house down in Kent."

I said, "won't that cost a fortune? I don't want to sound stingy but we're not millionaires."

Amanda wasted no time in saying, "we're both working, and I've already got some savings. They're sending me some quotes, so we can have a look. Sorry, I didn't mean to do it without telling you".

Amanda continued, "I just thought this place looked so nice, and it'll be great to treat your mum to a little bit of luxury. She could stay there for the weekend, they've got a spa and a swimming pool and beauty treatments."

I liked the sound of that, Amanda was right, my mum deserved to have a good time and to see me get married in church. A reception in lovely surroundings would make her so happy. "OK," I said, "who else would we invite?"

Amanda said, "well there's not many on my side, just an elderly aunt, a couple of distant cousins and some friends from work. You'll want Richard and Holly there I imagine and some of your colleagues, old school mates maybe?"

I said, "yeah there's one or two of my old mates I would like to see, if I can track them down that is."

Amanda turned and said, "there's always social media for that now, although be careful what you put out there or we're likely to have gate crashers turning up."

I said, "I don't suppose they'll bother going all that way just for a free drink, not some of the guys I'm thinking of!"

It was fun talking wedding stuff through with Amanda. I pictured my mum being there, including Holly and Richard, meeting my friends from work, all of them getting on together and having a good time. We went on to discuss what food we should have, and music. I told her about a guy I hadn't seen for years who a great DJ back then. Like Rich, he had been in trouble with the law, but he was basically a very decent person who'd had a rough time growing up. Rich would probably know where to find him and if we could help him out now—why not?"

There were others like him, who never had much of a chance in life. Why not invite them all to my fantastic wedding! From there, I started to dream about starting a charity, becoming one of those inner-city heroes who takes kids off the streets and turns them around. Richard could be a role model, going into schools, giving talks. Don't do drugs, get some smarts, to go college and all of that. I suppose I was in love and happy which it gave me a virtuous glow and the desire to make things right for the whole wide world.

It was now Saturday evening and Amanda and I had agreed to drive down to Kent to look at a country house the following day. We planned to stop and have lunch there, take our time and stroll around. The weather forecast for Sunday was good, and we were both looking forward to having a lovely day out. Amanda was, at that moment, preparing something delicious to eat. She was busy in the kitchen humming as she packed things to take along with us, we were both feeling in a holiday mood.

"I'm just slipping out to get a bottle of wine," I said, kissing her on the cheek as she tossed some olives into a bowl.

Amanda said, "there's some Sauvignon in the fridge."

"I don't think that'll last us, thirsty work this cooking lark."

Amanda laughed and popped an olive in my mouth, "how would you know!"

"Hi Karim, how are you?"

"Alright Jason, how are you today?"

Karim's family had kept the convenience store for years. You could buy almost anything there, his dad was always saying he had wanted to call the shop Harrods, but the owners of the name and brand wouldn't let him.

"How's the studies going," I asked, selecting a bottle from the shelf. Karim was studying law at university and had come home for the holidays to help-out in the store.

Karim grinned, "the law's an ass!" That's Dickens you know."

Just then, the door opened, and another customer came in. His face was drawn, his cheekbones showing through. He was also limping as he walked towards the counter. Mumbling something incoherent, he pointed at the tobacco and threw down some coins. Coughing heavily, he limped back to the door. When he had gone, Karim shook his head, "That guy shouldn't be smoking, he doesn't look well to me."

I asked, "do you know him, he seems familiar."

Karim said, "you've probably seen him around, I only know him by sight. He comes in whenever he has a couple of quid, only ever buys tobacco. But what can you do if he wants to kill himself? I did try talking to him once, but he didn't seem to hear me. I feel sorry him, you know what I mean. Maybe when I'm a hotshot lawyer I'll come back and sort his life out for him, if he'll let me."

So, I wasn't the only one with philanthropic impulses. The vague, virtuous daydream I had recently had about helping disadvantaged people, had returned. Karim was right. The guy did look in a bad way. Maybe he was homeless, had medical or some other kind of problem, and didn't know how to ask for help. There had to be a story there. On an impulse, I decided to follow him.

I had no trouble catching up with the man. He was still moving slowly toward the pedestrian crossing as I emerged from the store. Reaching the crossing at the same time, we stood side by side waiting for the light to change so we could cross the road. As it did so, I looked more closely at his face, I immediately recoiled in shock. There was no doubt about it, the limping man was Gareth.

31

Are You Sure It Was Him?

That night I could not sleep, the image of Gareth, limping, sick and feeble, would not leave my head. It seemed almost impossible to equate the person I had stood next to on the crossing, with the fit, strong, violent-tempered young man of whom we had all been afraid of when growing up. Me and my brother Richard, all the kids in the neighbourhood. But the face, though now wrinkled and thin, was unmistakable. There had been no sign of a gleaming Mercedes or any other car. After we had crossed the road, I had watched as Gareth continued to shuffle off slowly in the opposite direction.

I said nothing of the sighting to Amanda and Gareth's name had not come up in ages and because we had been having such a great evening, I hadn't wanted it to be taken over by speculation and discussion of this person who had figured so largely in both our lives. Yet for that very reason, I would have to tell her. I was also trying to analyse my own feelings. Seeing the once mighty Gareth reduced to a shambling, unkempt wreck had me shaken. Had fear been completely replaced by pity? Not quite! There was the fear that if I'd said hello, tried to be nice, that very act of common decency might be taken the wrong way. Gareth had always been a proud man and if the "kid" he had once intimidated had tried to get friendly, he might well think I was gloating. Was I? There was the possibility that he would turn on me, lashing out with his tongue if not his fists. He might even be carrying a knife and not be hesitant about using it. All these thoughts swirled about in my mind. Seeing Gareth had been one of those moments when one's inner world changes. The old order of things had shifted, and I was consumed with curiosity about the how and why of Gareth's downfall. Everyone grows old and wild young men are inevitably tamed by age and infirmity. But with Gareth, it seemed to have happened overnight. I wondered if Richard knew and what would Amanda's reaction be?

Amanda asked, "are you sure it was him?"

I replied, "I was standing right next to him."

It was Sunday morning and I had just returned from the corner shop with the papers. Amanda was making coffee, we were supposed to be getting ready to go to see the country house for our wedding reception, but instead the whole morning was taken up in conversation about Gareth.

Amanda said, "you didn't mention it when you came in."

I said, "well, you know, didn't want to spoil the evening."

Amanda looked thoughtful as she poured milk into the cups…and asked, "and did he see you?"

I said, "he looked in my direction, at one point, but he seemed quite glazed over. I'm pretty sure he didn't recognize me, or if he did, he was too stoned to make the connection."

Amanda put the coffees on the kitchen table and we both sat down and enquired, "and you say he looked ill?"

I shrugged, "I don't know about ill, but let's just say he didn't look in great shape. Remember, this guy was an athlete at school, he used to be in the gym every day, how old would he be now?"

Amanda thought for a moment, "thirty-ish, his birthday is in May."

"Well, the person I saw last night, I reckon anyone else would have taken him as a seventy-year-old man; and an unhealthy seventy-year-old at that."

Amanda frowned, "hard to take it in, isn't it? What do you think has happened to him?"

I shrugged, "either he's got some kind of disease or the drug taking has very quickly caught up with him, does he have family do you know?"

Amanda said, "none that he ever saw, I don't think, he never spoke to me about family. I've got a feeling his dad died when he was young; either that or he walked out on him and his mum."

I said, "a bit like you then."

Amanda responded, "yeah, a bit like the both of us really and if I remember correctly, he went off the rails for a while too just like me."

I replied, "I never meant any offence, but you got back on, that was quite sarcastic of you Amanda."

Amanda smiled and took my hand, "yes it was, but I now have you to thank for helping me."

I squeezed her hand in return, "you had strength of character, the willpower to live a decent life, Gareth always seemed too angry to want to change."

Amanda said, "I wonder if he has now?"

I said, "I wondered that too, how could we find out?"

Amanda and I looked at one another, thinking the same thought, Amanda spoke first, "we don't even know where he's living."

I said, "I assume its round here somewhere near the other side of Karim's shop, that seems to be his local. Karim says he comes in for tobacco quite regularly."

Amanda asked, "what else did Karim say about him?"

"Only that he felt a bit sorry for him and wished he could help him in some way," I said.

"Did you tell Karim you knew him?" Amanda asked.

I said, "no, the thing is, I wasn't sure if it was Gareth at that point. It didn't hit me until I went outside and stood next to him at the crossing. If Karim knew how that poor shuffling guy used to terrorize the community not so long ago, he'd be very surprised."

Amanda said, "well it's quite a surprise to me that he's even back in the area and an even bigger one to know that he's fallen on such hard times."

I said, "I know what you mean…if someone had told me Gareth was in prison or living in a massive house somewhere, or had gone to Spain or LA, or even that he had been shot dead, I wouldn't have been surprised. But to just go downhill like that so quickly, it's the last thing I would have expected."

"There but for the grace of God go I," sighed Amanda… "are you going to try to speak to him?"

"Me? Why?" I asked.

Amanda said, "I don't know, I just got the impression you felt sorry for him, like Karim did."

"Hmm, I suppose I do, but would he want me being a do-gooder and poking my nose in his business? Could it be that he doesn't want anyone's help?"

"That's a good point," conceded Amanda… "it might do more harm than good, maybe it's best to let sleeping dogs lie."

We sipped our coffee in silence for a moment, each of us thinking about Gareth,

Was doing nothing the right thing to do, I wondered?

I said, "I suppose there's no way of knowing whether to offer help, if we don't know more about his circumstances. In fact, at this present moment, we don't know anything."

"Another good point honey, for all we know, he could very well be living in that big house you mentioned," Amanda said.

"With a supermodel girlfriend and servants," I said.

Amanda pipped in, "and a ton of money in the bank from all his drug deals."

I said, "then again, he would probably send one of the servants out to buy his tobacco. And his clothes wouldn't be full of holes like the ones I saw him in last night," we both laughed.

Amanda said, "that's true actually…Gareth was always into clothes."

I nodded, "I remember him wearing all the designer labels, I always thought he never bought any of them. My brother Richard almost got into trouble big time, for going with him on a warehouse job one night."

Amanda said, "I remember that, gosh, it seems like years ago, doesn't it?"

I said, "sure does, Richard's a changed man now, thank God.... after a long pause, I asked, "I wonder if Gareth is?"

Amanda asked, "do we really care? I don't mean that to sound unkind. As a matter of fact, I do care. That is… oh, I don't know what I think really, it's like the past is catching up with the both of us. You know, you seeing him like that, the whole thing has just thrown me a bit."

I said, "likewise, maybe it's best to do nothing until we know more. It might turn out that Gareth's married, or living with someone. He may even be just passing through the area."

Amanda said, "that's true, he was never one to settle in any place for too long."

I took Amanda's hand affectionately and I said, "let's move on. We've got a wedding to plan, remember?" The look in her eyes told me she was as excited and happy as I was, and it felt really good.

32

~~~~~~

■ Wedding Planners

"Currently, we can accommodate up to thirty wedding guests for that particular night madam." The manager looked up from his computer screen and smiled and continued to say, "hotel guests also have free access to our health spa, heated indoor swimming pool and jacuzzi. Plus, generous discounts on our full range of beauty treatments."

Amanda and I had travelled to Kent to check out the country house she had mentioned. It was a 16th Century Coach Inn with converted stables, set in beautiful gardens, the place was certainly impressive!

I said to Amanda, as we strolled back to the car, "if we do get married here, my mum will think we've won the lottery."

Amanda said, "I know but actually, the prices he's quoted aren't too bad at all, what do you think?"

I responded, "I think it's a fantastic venue and I agree that the hire charge is quite reasonable. And I guess the people we invite from work, will expect to pay for their own rooms, if they expect to stay overnight."

Amanda said, "so, is that a yes?"

I smiled, "it's a maybe, all right, a probably, we're only going to get married once, so why not do it in style."

"Oh Jason! Yes! Yes! Yes! It's going to be fantastic! I do love you so."

I said, "it will mean budgeting carefully over the next few months."

Amanda said, "absolutely honey, whatever you say!"

I said…"and as for that honeymoon in Hawaii…"

Amanda said, "forget that but we will go somewhere nice?"

I said, "how does a weekend in Margate sound?"

Amanda responded, "blissful."

On the drive back to London I thought about how lucky Amanda and I were. Head over heels in love, both in good jobs, a nice home and now we were planning a wedding in a luxury venue. I couldn't help myself thinking how there were people around the world who were starving, homeless, in need of basic necessities; people who would think it a luxury just to be safe and have enough to eat. Even in our own country there was hunger and deprivation, and those who had lost their way in life. Was it a mere coincidence that just as I was having these thoughts, I saw Gareth again?

"Why are you stopping here?" Amanda asked. We were a few streets from home, I had pulled over on the curb.

"Gareth," I said

Amanda said, "what?"

I responded, "on the other side of the road, look."

Amanda peered in the direction I was pointing, she drew in her breath. "You have got to be kidding me!"

I said, "uh, uh! He was wearing that same coat the other night too."

Amanda said, "oh, my goodness, he doesn't look well at all."

I said, "looks like he's heading for the shop…so he must be living some-where quite nearby."

Amanda said, "Yes. Oh well! There but for the grace of God, as you say," and then sighed and shook her head, "come on Jason, let's go home."

The following day we were in church, sitting beside us in the congregation were my mum, my brother Richard and Holly. As we were waiting for the service to begin, Richard leaned towards me.

"So, is it true what Mum said," he asked. "That you two are getting hitched?"

"Richard!" said my mum in a loud whisper, "don't you use such a common expression, especially not in church."

"Of course, it's true," I said, "when has our mother ever lied to either of us? And don't worry, you're all invited. In fact, Richard, you're going to be my best man."

Holly looked pleased and reached over and gave my arm a little squeeze. "God bless you both, Richard, you know you're going to have to make a speech."

Richard looked momentarily horrified, "really?"

"It is traditional," I said.

"But what am I going to say," Richard asked.

My mum started laughing, "don't worry son, you've got nearly a year to think about it!"

"You have to tell everyone what a great guy the groom is and how he's always been there for you," said Holly.

"In short, just tell the truth," I grinned.

"Oh, and to amuse the wedding guests, you also have to tell a couple of embarrassing stories," added Holly.

"Embarrassing to me, not to you," I said.

"Shush! Right now, you're both embarrassing me," said Mum.

The service began with an address followed by a hymn after which, a member of the congregation got up and recited a parable. It was the story of the Good Shepherd.

"…And this shepherd had in his flock one hundred sheep, and when he counted them, he found that there but ninety-nine. So, he left the ninety-nine and went in search of the one that was lost. He searched and searched over the hills and valleys and fields and mountains, growing weary and hungry, but thinking only of his quest and how hungry and weary that poor lost sheep must be. And when eventually he found the sheep he called out to his friends and neighbours and said, "Rejoice with me, for I have found my lost sheep. And I tell you, there will be more rejoicing in heaven over one sinner who repents than over ninety-nine righteous persons…"

Amanda, who had been very quiet since we arrived, was following the sermon attentively. As we left the church and made our way home, she seemed wrapped in thought. The sermon had got me thinking too. There was not just one lost sheep out there. As I reflected, I realized there were hundreds, thousands, too many to count. Amanda herself had been one, so had Richard. And here we all were now, going to church and living good, useful lives. But was it enough? A sense of guilt about my good fortune seemed to haunt me from time to time, perhaps a lot of people felt like that.

The following evening, on the way home from work, I went to Karim's corner shop to buy some milk. As I approached, I saw a thin, bedraggled figure in the doorway. It was Gareth. I decided to hang back until he had gone. As I waited in the shadows another figure emerged from the shop carrying a bag laden with groceries. It was Amanda. About to join her I suddenly hesitated, as I saw her take Gareth's arm in a caring gesture. I then watched spellbound as Amanda guided him slowly towards the curb and helped him into her car, a moment later they had driven off together.

33

▪One Lost Sheep

I stood blinking into the darkness trying to interpret what I had just seen. Well, it was obvious, I supposed. Amanda had bumped into Gareth in the shop and feeling sorry for him, had bought him some groceries. Seeing he had difficulty walking she had then offered him a lift home. It was odd though, as Amanda didn't usually visit the corner shop on a weekday. Had she gone there looking for Gareth? Oh well! I thought, what if she had? It was perfectly understandable. I had still been toying with the idea myself, of trying to do something for him; if only by anonymously alerting Social Services that there was a guy who might be in need of their help. Well, Amanda would know his address now and about his living conditions, so we could talk that over together.

As I was getting the milk, Karim mentioned that Amanda had been in the shop just a few minutes earlier. "Looks like you're in for a good night," he winked. "We only see your other half in here on the weekends as a rule."

I said, "what do you mean a good night?"

"Well, she bought steak, fresh cream, wine… sorry man. I've probably spoiled her big surprise now", Karim said.

"That's all right," I smiled, "I won't let on and I'll still look surprised."

 So, the bag of groceries had been for us, or had it?

When I arrived at the flat the lights were off and there was no sign of Amanda's car. I put some music on, poured a drink and flopped onto the sofa. It was another half an hour before Amanda appeared. There was no bag of groceries, she leaned over the back of the sofa and kissed me.

"Stuck in traffic?" I said.

She hesitated for a millisecond, "not really."

"Not really," was my response.

"I thought we'd phone for a takeaway tonight if that's ok, your favourite Indian," she said.

I said, "you know me, I never say no to a curry, drink?"

"That's all right I'll get it," Amanda said.

"So how was your day?" I asked.

"Oh, so-so," Amanda replied.

"Nothing out of the ordinary," I enquired.

"Budget reports, area management inspection and a new intern started, how about you?"

I said, "oh, so-so."

Amanda laughed and took out her phone, "you are funny, now, do you want rice or naan bread?"

I said, "both."

Amanda quickly replied, "greedy."

After we had eaten, I said, "I saw you at the shop earlier this evening."

Amanda froze, "oh!"

"And I saw Gareth."

Amanda quickly said, "I was going to tell you, I swear."

"But not straightaway," I replied.

Amanda said, "I thought you'd be upset…are you?"

I said, "only that you didn't tell me…but yes, I do understand why…did Gareth enjoy the steak?"

Then Amanda asked, "how did you know?"

I said, "Karim."

"He doesn't miss a trick," Amanda replied.

I said, "no, I imagine he'll be an excellent lawyer, but he'll need to be more discreet with his clients' information."

Amanda gave a big sigh and poured herself another drink, "I suppose I'd better give you all the details."

I said, "I have to admit I am curious."

Amanda said, "as we both suspected, Gareth is living alone and not doing very well for himself."

"I take it he's on benefits."

Amanda shared, "I didn't ask, but I would assume so. He's got a flat on Lowell Road, it's pretty dingy, second-hand furniture and bare floorboards."

I decided to ask, "what's the story with his limp?"

Then Amanda said, "he smashed up his Mercedes some time ago and was in the hospital for a couple of weeks. His leg never recovered properly and he's in pain most of the time."

I then asked, "is there anyone else in his life? Did he mention family, a girlfriend?"

Amanda responded, "no, I don't think so, he didn't say that much. I just cooked him a good healthy meal and sat with him while he ate it. He really seemed to appreciate it, I don't think he looks after himself properly, the smoking doesn't help. He's changed though Jason, really changed."

"Coming down in the world does that to people," I said.

Amanda replied, "and he's certainly come down, he doesn't seem to have any friends."

I said, well he's got one now."

Amanda looked at me, trying to gauge whether I was being sarcastic or not. I wasn't even sure myself. I was also wondering if this was a one-off act of charity on Amanda's part, or was she intending to adopt Gareth in some way? Doubtless she didn't know the answer to that herself. Either way, I realized I had no right to dictate to her. What made me uncomfortable of course, was the fact that this was not just anyone she had helped. This was Gareth, someone who'd done bad things to other people, someone who led my brother astray, the man whom Amanda had once lived with and at one time, professed to love.

I decided to take the initiative. "Maybe we should try to help him on a regular basis…what do you think?" Amanda frowned, "it's very difficult to understand how much help we can offer and what kind of help we can offer. There are practical things we could do, sure, and I know your mum would suggest inviting him along to church."

"That might do more harm than good," I warned her…"remember how he hated religion?"

"I was about to say the same thing, no, he would only resent us," Amanda said.

"One question," I said, "did you tell him about us, that we are still together and getting married?"

"Yes, I told him that straightaway, I didn't want there to be any misunderstanding on that score as to why I was there."

I asked, "what did he say?"

Amanda responded, "nothing really, he seemed so out of it. He just nodded and murmured something like, "right, right." It didn't seem to annoy him in any way, he seems completely beyond anger." I had no reason to doubt Amanda and her words made me feel so much better. What reason did I have to be jealous of anyone, least of all a sick man: someone who needed our help and sympathy above all else?

"I do love you, Amanda."

"And I love you too, Jason."

34

▪ What Do You Want?

I knocked on the door again, a little harder this time. After about half a minute I heard shuffling from within, then the rattling of bolts. The door, which was held by a security chain on the inside, creaked open a couple of inches. A pair of bloodshot eyes peered out and a wheezing voice said, "Bible Boy."

Amanda had given me Gareth's address, but it had taken me three days before I decided to pay him a visit. Even now, I don't know what possessed me to do it. It was obviously a mystery to Gareth too.

"What do you want," Gareth said.

I responded with, "I'm sorry to intrude Gareth, tell me to go away if you like."

Gareth quickly replied, "I'm thinking about it," he wheezed again, coughed loudly and swallowed hard.

I then said, "Amanda told me that you had an accident."

"That's history man…so, what do you want?" Gareth said.

I responded by saying, "just to ask if there's anything I can do."

In a course tone Gareth said, "Like what?"

I shrugged, "I don't know really, is there anything you need?"

Gareth with his irritable self said, "what, like God?"

I said, "I know you better than that," this brought a wry smile to Gareth's grizzled features.

Gareth said, "I need money."

I hesitated then said, "for food and stuff?"

Then Gareth said, "what's it to you Bible Boy? You asked what I needed, and I told you, if you're not rich enough to look big, then on your way mate!"

Taking out my wallet, I found a twenty-pound note and put it through the narrow crack in the door, and I said, "here, please take this."

Gareth pressed the note to his lips, "thanks," he growled.....
"I always knew you were alright. No hard feelings for what went on in days gone by, eh?"

"Oh no, no," I stammered, "just so long as you're alright, that's all."

Gareth gave a hacking laugh, "do I look alright? Do I sound alright? Get real!"

I said, "well, like I say, if there is anything else you need..."

Gareth replied, "yeah, I'll tell you what else I need."

I said, "what?"

Then Gareth said, "when you're done with my woman, just send her back to me will you?"

I responded with, "Sorry?"

Gareth with a sharp tone said, "you heard,...and there's no need to be sorry, just tell her I'm waiting and there's no hard feelings."

Gareth's eyes had fixed me in a mesmerising stare from which I found it very hard to look away.

I murmured, "I had better go now," and was about to say, "good to see you" but stopped myself just in time. Gareth quickly interjected and said, "thank you, Bible Boy," in a hard but polite voice that bordered on mocking and then he slammed the door shut.

When I returned to the flat, Amanda switched off the TV and looked up from the sofa. I went to and filled the coffee machine, I needed caffeine or maybe something stronger.

"Hello darling, it was a bit of a non-event really," I said. "Unlike you, I wasn't invited in. Other than that, he seems much the same old Gareth, cynical, haughty; just obviously a little vulnerable, on the physical side."

"Yes, that was the impression I got too," Amanda said, as she lifted a cushion and put it behind her head. "I don't think we'll be getting him along to church anytime soon. Still at least you've been round and done your duty as a good Christian."

I replied, "I don't know about that, but it was certainly playing on my mind. I couldn't rest until I'd been there, just to show I was willing, do you know what I mean?"

Amanda responded, "uh huh."

Then I said, "he must feel lonely though, underneath that bravado."

Amanda interjected, "oh, I'm sure too, but he's not going to show weakness to you of all people."

"Not to any man I would imagine," I said.

Amanda quickly said, "you know it's funny though."

I said, "what is?"

I poured two coffees, handed one to Amanda and sat beside her on the sofa.

"The thing I said just now, about not getting Gareth into church, do you think there's a possibility, is that what you're saying?"

Amanda leaned forward, her eyes bright, her expression intense, "it's just that people would have said that about me at one time, wouldn't they?"

I interjected, "that you'd never go near a church?"

Amanda replied, "exactly, and now there I am every Sunday, with my lovely fiancé, praising the Lord, singing hymns, praying and saying Amen."

I said, "ah, but you started out as a good Christian." "You had your difficulties and your challenges, and you came through that trial. Gareth never had the same start in life, he has nothing good to reference or use as a guide for his life."

Amanda nodded earnestly, "you're right, I mean, who were his role models?"

I said, "Al Capone probably!"

Amanda laughed, "probably, Gareth would have done well in Chicago."

I said, "he'd have died young, he probably will anyway."

Her tone serious now, Amanda said, "that thought crossed my mind too."

"Amanda, Gareth said something to me that really disturbed me. He said, "when you're done with my woman, just send her back to me will you?" If he wasn't so frail, I would have punched him."

"Don't let him get into your mind, Jason, he knows how to play mind games.

"Amanda, be very careful around him, do you hear me, be very careful!"

35

▪️I Never Saw it Coming

A few weeks had passed, and I started to notice that Amanda was carrying out more and more humanitarian tasks for Gareth. The visits had gone from being one visit a week to two, sometimes even three. One day after coming home from work I called out to her, "Amanda, Amanda, where are you", there was no answer.

I took my shoes off and went upstairs, she would sometimes have a brief nap on the bed after coming in from work but on this day, there was no Amanda. Not to worry; she had obviously been held up at work, so I went downstairs again and began preparing dinner. Funny she hadn't rung or texted through yet, she usually did.

An hour later and there was still no word, I had now sent Amanda a few text messages and left a voicemail asking what time she might be in but so far, there had been no reply. I unconvincingly kept telling myself that the reception could be patchy on the underground. I then decided to have a glass of wine and give it another fifteen minutes or so. Finding there was no wine in the flat, I put on my coat and headed at a brisk walk to the corner shop, where I was greeted by Karim, "Hello stranger."

"Hi Karim, how are you?" I placed the bottle of white wine on the counter.

Karim smiled, "Very well thanks! Hey, you two are drinking fast tonight, or are you having a party?"

I was perplexed and said, "sorry, what do you mean?"

Then Karim said, "your good lady was in here only about twenty minutes ago."

I responded, "Amanda?"

"How many good ladies have you got," Karim said.

Still feeling confused, I said, "Amanda was in here twenty minutes ago?"

Karim said, "yeah, that's what I just said, bought two bottles of wine, hey, what's wrong?"

Then I said, "it's just that she's not been home yet."

Karim responded with, "oh."

"Keep the change," I said laying a ten-pound note on the counter, I hurried out of the shop, calling Amanda's mobile on the way.

My worst fear was that something had happened to Amanda between the shop and home. When she finally answered my call, that fear was allayed, she was with Gareth. My relief was immediately replaced by a numbing distress. This had been my second fear and one that had lain at the back of my mind ever since we had known Gareth was back living in the area. The fact that Amanda sounded drunk when she answered the phone didn't help my state of mind. It was now 10.00pm, and she said she would be home very soon…how soon? I was now angry as well as upset. She launched into an apologetic speech, saying how worried she had been about Gareth living all on his own, and how she just felt she ought to spend a bit of time with him. She sounded very guilty and very torn. "OK," I told her, "I'll come "round and walk you back because it's late."

When I arrived, Amanda was already at the door and there was no sign of Gareth. She was unsteady on her feet and the smell of cannabis was wafting from inside. Back home Amanda cried a little and uttered profuse apologies as I helped her up to bed. The next morning, she had gone and there was a note on the kitchen table:

My Darling Jason,

This is to let you know I am going to be spending a few days by myself out of town, as I am having such a difficult time right now. It's as though my old life is trying to resurrect itself and right now, I don't feel strong enough to cope with my thoughts and my emotions.

I know this is very hard on you and I am sorry. I just feel that I am being torn between you and Gareth. He has no one in his life at the moment and is in a bad way. He needs help and I might be the help that he needs. I know you love me, and I truly do love you too,

Oh, I am so confused right now!

Jason, I am so sorry, but this won't be forever, I do want to marry you, I really do but Gareth still has a part of me attached to him and a part of me just seems not to want to let go. Not right now anyway, I hope you understand. I am in a bad place right now and this is something I have to work through.

Please forgive me.

All my love, Amanda

I stared at the note, trying to make sense of it, trying to work out what was really happening, and why. My throat was dry, my palms were sweating, I could feel my heart racing. I dropped down onto the bed, my head swimming with so many thoughts as to WHY... and what I should or even could do, to change things.

"I know, I will call my mum and ask for her advice." Or was it that I simply needed to hear her voice, to hear words of comfort and reassurance? Then I thought, maybe I'm overreacting, and this really is just something Amanda needs to get out of her system. But what do I do in the meantime?

Everything felt so unstable, as if the ground were sinking beneath me. Should I go around to Gareth's to find out where Amanda was staying? It might make things worse, but then what was the alternative? To just sit and wait for her to return? In the end that was all I could do. I just had to wait.

A few days became a fortnight, then a month and still there was no word from Amanda. My calls and texts went unanswered and I grew increasingly depressed. Work and routine kept me sane, but only just and in the evenings, I tried to go out as much as possible. To the cinema, the library... wherever I could find solace. People of course, were wondering where Amanda was, as she had not shown her face since the morning she left the flat. For a while I took to hanging around the corner shop or outside Gareth's flat, but on each occasion, there had been no sign of either of them. My mum and Richard were sympathetic but like me, had no idea what, if anything, could be done about the situation.

Six months went by and I had resigned myself to the fact that Amanda wasn't coming back. I wasn't even sure that she and Gareth were still living in the area, as I still hadn't seen either of them. Maybe they had gone up north together; to one of Gareth's old haunts.

Although accepting my fate, I wasn't in any way happy or even relieved about it. Various friends suggested that I try to meet someone else and on one desperate occasion, I even agreed to a blind date. Not that I had any desire for it to work out. Meanwhile, all my thoughts focused on one thing, what on earth would become of Amanda?

36

▪ Too Many Questions and No Answers

I had always struggled to understand why something so perfect could end so suddenly and so abruptly. Ever since my childhood, I've pondered on how this coffee-coloured girl with the green eyes had entered my world. It was a bright sunny day when her family moved into the area. She looked happy, her mum and Dad also looked happy, but something changed in their house that also changed Amanda. I witnessed her growing up, making bad decision after bad decision and now it appears as if history was repeating itself. I remember planning my wedding with Amanda and during that brief time with her, everything seemed perfect. It was as though I was living in a perfect world, looking at everything through rose-coloured glasses.

Did she truly love me as I loved her? Was she really free from the clutches of drug and alcohol abuse? Was it that her father, who hadn't played a major role in her life, was a deciding factor in how she understood what it meant to be loved? So many questions and no one to answer them. I was living in torment and with no knowledge of what happened to Amanda.

Oftentimes I would pick up the last note that Amanda left, re-reading it and trying to make sense of it; decipher the true meaning of the words. I had no peace and wanted to know why it was that Amanda's troubled past was now affecting my present, I wanted my joy and my happiness back.

What was it that drew her to Gareth, was she desperately trying to get him to become a Christian? I have seen so many women leave church then find themselves in abusive relationships, no longer wanting God or anything to do with the church. My Amanda it appears, has become another statistic, another soul who got off the operating table while surgery was still taking place.

For my own peace, I had to find out what had happened to her. I woke up one Saturday morning and decided to take a trip to Manchester. I was determined that I would find Amanda and when I did, I was going to sit her down and make her see reality.

I purchased an expensive ticket, I would have got it cheaper if I'd pre-booked, but this was all done on a whim, I had to find Amanda. Even though I didn't really know what I was really doing, I boarded the train and sat in my seat, I rode quietly and tried to enjoy the journey. To my surprise, more and more people started to fill the carriage and I was disappointed. Beer drinking football fans were in the carriage with me and for four hours, I had to listen to just about every football song you could have imagined; the noise was relentless.

I booked myself into a hotel and slept, the journey had left me exhausted. I knew that in the morning my quest to find Amanda would begin. On the following, day I set out to see if I could find her, I hadn't realized that Manchester was such a big place.

My first plan of action was to go to a hostel and begin to ask questions about the services provided for the homeless, alcoholics and drug users. The hostel, receptionist was very helpful, I left with more leaflets and information than you could imagine. That evening, I started trawling through the leaflets, trying to find anything that would be of use. I wanted to gather information so I could start to make phone calls, send emails or even attend any of the hostels listed on the leaflets. It was a task I was dreading but the next morning I got up, had a bite to eat then started to make phone call after phone call. By about midday, I had given up as it was a bigger task than I was ready for. What I was attempting to do was the impossible; how on earth am I going to find Amanda? It was like looking for a needle in a haystack.

I laid on the bed in my hotel room and as I was about to take a nap, I had a thought.

"I know" I said to myself, "I'll try to retrace her steps from some of the stories she told me and try to retrace her steps from some of the places she described to me. Hopefully some of the places will be close by."

Amanda once told me about the time when she was homeless and hungry and how, being desperate for something to eat she had stopped at a café and ordered food, knowing full well that she had no money to pay for it. She'd mentioned the name of the cafe but for the life of me, I couldn't remember what it was.

When the food arrived, Amanda said, she wolfed it down and was prepared to accept whatever the Café owners were going to do to her, she was hungry and didn't care. She said if they beat her up it wouldn't matter, she was too hungry to care. After she had taken the last mouthful of food and had sipped the last drop of tea from the white enamel mug, she burped loudly, which drew a lot of attention to her. Amanda said was quite thin and had lost a lot of weight, her oversized clothes made it obvious that she was living rough. One by one, as the faces had turned away from her in disgust, Amanda stared at them, swearing, while telling them to mind their own business. Then as the door opened and another customer came in, Amanda headed for the door, almost knocking over the woman who was trying to enter the café.

"Hey!" the waitress shouted, "come back here!"

It was too late Amanda was hot-footing it down the road.

The waitress with a raised voice, "Geoff, that homeless woman has just run off!"

Geoff replied, "who the lady that ate by the window?"

The waitress responded, "yes, the homeless looking woman."

Geoff asked, "which way did she go?" Before Geoff had even finished his sentence, he too was off, running down the road chasing after Amanda.

It wasn't long before he had grabbed the tail of her coat, causing her to trip and fall to the ground. As she did, he grabbed her, and a tussle began between the two of them. Amanda seemed to be fighting for her life, while Geoff was just standing there holding her firmly by her coat so that she wouldn't get away.

Geoff said to Amanda, "hey lady calm down."

As a torrent of abuse started to leave Amanda's mouth, Geoff shouted all the louder.

Geoff's response to Amanda, "hey lady, calm down, I am not going to hurt you."

Then Amanda said, "what do you want, I have no money but if it's sex that you want, then let's go, I can pay for my food that way."

Geoff replied, "lady!"

Amanda's response to Geoff, "don't call me lady, I ain't no lady!"

Geoff said, "Madam."

At this point Amanda started to chuckle, "Madam indeed, you might as well call me that. That name seems to have stuck."

Geoff then said to Amanda in a calm soothing Mediterranean accent, "look, I don't know what you are talking about, but you ran off without paying for your meal, that is not nice." Geoff continue to talk to Amanda, "if you were hungry, we could have fed you, given you a sandwich or something."

"You can let me go now," said Amanda.

Geoff said, "sorry I never realized I was holding you so tight, I hope I haven't hurt you. Look, we need someone who can help out at the café, if you need food, we can pay you with meals."

37

The Princess Starts Her New Job

The following day after agreeing to work at the café, Amanda strolled in looking scruffy and unkempt. The first thing her new employer did, was to order her to have a wash. She was given the key to the flat above the café and she opened the door to a warm, cosy and well decorated flat. She made her way to the bathroom and tidied herself up. Still wearing the same oversized clothes but looking a lot cleaner, Amanda re-entered the café, ready to start her first day at work. Geoff gave her an apron that hid the unwashed and stained clothes she was wearing, and she began to wash plate after plate. Amanda told me that she couldn't wait for the day to end and that it was one of the worst things she had ever had to do. At the end of that first day Geoff put three hundred and fifty pounds in Amanda's hand and told her to buy some new clothes. As she was leaving, he asked her if she had somewhere to stay, when Amanda said no, Geoff offered to let her use the flat upstairs for free.

Amanda enquired, "why are you being so nice to me? What do you want from me?"

Geoff replied, "Princess I want nothing."

Amanda, snapped, "don't you dare call me Princess. Don't you ever call me that! In fact, you can stick your job. I ain't coming back!" She slammed the door shut, almost shattering the glass.

I can remember when Amanda told me the story, I could almost see Amanda's nostrils flaring as she told Geoff what to do with his job it amused me so much, I couldn't help but laugh. You can imagine that it didn't go down too well, Amanda definitely didn't find it funny.

Like I said, I couldn't remember the name of the café but remembered Amanda telling me that it was near a building that had a large illuminated sign on it.

"THE METROPOLIS! YES, that's what it is, it's called, The Metropolis!"

I opened my tablet and started searching for "Metropolis, Manchester." It didn't take long until I found it. It was called the Metropolis Apartments and my task for tomorrow was to head down to the Metropolis Apartments and find Amanda.

The next day couldn't come soon enough, I thought if I went to bed early it might help. So, I was in bed by 9:00 pm but couldn't sleep. I was more anxious than ever, it seems my trip to Manchester wasn't in vain. I woke up the next morning and quickly washed, got dressed and went for breakfast. While eating my toasted marmalade sandwich, I began to daydream. My thoughts were now directed back to one of the other stories Amanda had told me, "Jason, there's something that I need to tell you."

My heart now racing with anxiety, I tried to appear as calm as I could as I responded,

"yes darling, I`m listening."

Then Amanda started to share that while in Manchester, "I did go back to the cafe and I apologised to Geoff. I had calmed down and told him why I'd had the outburst".

We were in the flat above the cafe talking and I was so relaxed that I found it easy to share my life with him. Perhaps I just needed someone to listen to me. Geoff was a good listener, he sat opposite from me on one sofa and I sat on the other and recounted my story.

Apart from you, he was the only other person that has seen me cry so much. I hadn't cried so much in a long time, I poured my heart out to him. I told him about my father who watched me playing dress-up in my mother's room; trying on her high-heeled shoes, hats and coats. I told him how my dad called me his little Princess. Then one day, I saw him walk out on me, only to remarry and have himself another Princess.

As Amanda told me the story, all I could do was weep with her.

"Jason, are you crying?" Amanda said.

"Who me? Never, it's hay fever," I said to her, "please continue."

"Geoff was so sweet to me, he was a real gentleman. He let me stay in the flat and never charged me a penny. He even gave me my old job back. What was strange at first though, was the fact that he was such a handsome man who never talked about a wife or girlfriend and he never made a pass at me either. As time passed, we became good friends and would often have a drink and a smoke but nothing too heavy. Then one day he switched on me as we were hanging out in the flat. He became very aggressive towards me and started demanding sex from me. He kept telling me it was unpaid rent and food. At that point I became scared and headed for the door to see if I could get away. The next minute I was pinned to the door, then he started punching me in the face, I was brutally raped. The most sickening part of it was that he kept calling me his little Princess. Jason, you're crying, here, wipe your tears."

As I sat eating my breakfast, I suddenly felt such an urgency to find the Metropolis Apartments, what was it about Amanda?

For as long as I have known her, all I ever wanted was for her to be my love. I would have made her happy, but she never saw that in me. Deception and lies always seemed to cloud Amanda's understanding of love. Why was it that she always went looking for love in the wrong place?

38

The Metropolis Building

When I first arrived in Manchester, I was tired as the journey exhausting, but now I was angry. I was hurt too because my best friend had been abused and as much as I wanted to help, there was nothing I could have done to change the course of events. It seemed like Amanda's life choices had sealed her fate.

I was hurt because she had walked out on me, walked out on God, walked out on her future, and walked out on every promise we had made to each other. Yes, I was heartbroken, but I was also a lot stronger now.

"That will be twelve pounds please sir," said the cab driver, he sounded like Bob Hoskins. I could barely make out what he was saying

"How Much?" I said.

"Twelve pounds and the Metropolis Apartments is just over there," said the cab driver.

As I walked with trepidation towards the building, I kept reciting to myself, "fear not, for the Lord thy God is with you," I needed the encouragement. As I turned the corner, I could see the café Amanda had described, it was boarded up with a for sale sign hung on the outside, I was devastated! In fact, words couldn't describe how I felt, I wanted to give up.

I took down the number of the real estate agent selling the property and called, hoping I could get information on the vendor. The agent reminded me of Karim, my singing canary friend who could tell you everything that happened in and around the area I lived in. Within minutes of talking to the agent I had the owners' phone number and business address and lo and behold, it was Geoff; Geoff the rapist.

I don't know what I did to persuade him to give me the details but whatever it was, it was a God-send. I called the number and a gentleman answered the phone, "good morning Sir, my name is Jason and I'm interested in buying your property can we meet up?"

"Hi Jason, by all means, I am free now, on arrival, please see the receptionist, who is my wife, she will settle you in."

"Taxi! Taxi! I need to go to the following address and I need to be there NOW!"

When I arrived, I was met by one of the most attractive women I had ever seen, she was gorgeous!

"Hello, I'm Maria and you must be Jason, we were expecting you."

I said, "thank you so much, yes I am Jason and I have come to see your husband about the property. You must be a very lucky woman to have such a faithful husband."

"Yes, he's adorable," Maria replied.

"And so charitable," I said to Maria.

Maria looked at me with a look of sheer confusion then quickly called for Geoff.

"Geoff, you have a visitor."

"Hi Jason, how can I help you?"

I said, "I am looking for a friend of mine." As I began to describe Amanda, Maria suddenly screamed, "she's that crazy alcoholic druggy that threatened to kill me and slit my children's throats. What is this and what does my husband have to do with her?"

Geoff's tanned look had disappeared, he was now virtually crimson in colour.

"I think you had better go," Geoff said.

"Please, tell me where I can find her?" I asked in desperation.

By this time a hysterical Maria screamed, "she is staying in the hostel on South Street, now get out!"

 As I left the building, I could hear screaming and shouting, Maria was demanding answers.

I was brought up in a Christian home and was taught that we ought to forgive. I was told that the battle isn't ours, but the Lord's. Well, on that day I saw God at work, you can call it karma, but I know what it meant to me.

39

Why Amanda? Why?

I had no time to waste, I was heading down to South Street to find my soulmate.

The taxi driver never stopped talking for the duration of the ride, but to be truthful, I never heard a word he said, the whole journey was a blur.

"That will be twelve pounds please," said the cab driver.

"How much?" I asked, "this must be some kind of a joke," I whispered to myself.

"I said twelve pounds," the taxi driver said.

I replied, "the last taxi cost me exactly the same amount."

The taxi driver retorted, "and your point is?"

In frustration I said, "look, I'm in a rush so keep the change."

As I approached the door of the hostel, I caught sight of the shape of someone that was familiar to me. "That person looks like Amanda," I said to myself.

"Amanda!" I shouted from across the road, the person's head turned suddenly and looked up. It was Amanda but the first thing I noticed was a deep scar across her face.

"Amanda, it's me Jason." She screamed and ran out of the building, I ran after her and grabbing her arm, shouted at her to stop. She'd lost a lot of weight; her teeth weren't clean, and her hair was matted, she was a mess.

I said out of concern, "what's happened to you?"

"**** off Jason! I am not Amanda, I'm Mandy and if you don't want to get hurt, you'd, better go. Gareth has threatened that the next time he sees you, it'll either be you or me."

"I am not afraid of Gareth," I said.

Amanda snapped, "well I am, look at what he's done to me…he slit my face wide open when I was sleeping and poured boiling water all over me."

I pleaded, "come back to London with me….I promise you I will protect you."

Amanda shrieked, "Bible basher, you seem to have forgotten that you're a mummy's boy, you can't protect nothing."

I just said, "Amanda, that doesn't faze me anymore, I am more concerned about your wellbeing."

Amanda, wailed, "look, bugger off, I ain't interested anymore, you're all the same, every one of you, from my dad down to you."

Gareth seemed to appear from nowhere and shouted, "Mandy, who are you talking to? Ah, it's the mummy's boy from London. Boy, haven't I told you already to leave my woman alone?" In the blink of an eye, Gareth had slapped Amanda in the face. I immediately reacted by grabbing him by his lapels, drawing his face as close to mine as I could. As I gritted my teeth, I warned him that the next time he would be dead if he so much as sneezed near her.

"Sir, if you don't let him go, I am going to call the police," said a bystander.

As I released Gareth from my grip, I looked at him, pointing my finger at him in disgust. I picked up Amanda and forcefully carried her away, saying, "Amanda, why, why, why, why have you done this to yourself?"

Amanda, pleaded, "leave me alone, you're hurting me and you're going to make things worse for me."

I said in a concerned tone, "take out a restraining order on him; he won't be able to get near you."

All I want to know Amanda is why, why did you walk out on our bright future, you broke my heart again!"

Then Amanda said, "Jason, I thought I was strong, but Gareth kept feeding me with alcohol and drugs and he kept reminding me about the good times we had, I got drawn in. Just like the Jekyll and Hyde character that he is, he changed and started beating me up, threatening to kill me. He never forgave me for being with you, as far as he was concerned, I was always his girl and I had been cheating on him with you. When I plucked up the courage to say I was going back to London, he slit my face with a knife and continued to abuse me. How did you find me?"

I replied, "I remembered the story you told me about Geoff, I tracked him down, both him and his wife. I heard you threatened his wife and his children, what was that all about?"

"It's too long a story to tell" Amanda said, "but let's just say, it was payback and more for what he did to me, I was high on drugs at the time."

Seemingly, from nowhere, Gareth piped up, "Mandy, what did I tell you about talking to that little boy? I came looking for you and where do I find you, talking to him, I warned you before but this time you're dead!"

Gareth marched towards us like a man on a mission and it was then I saw red and punched him square on the nose. Blood flowed like a fountain and it felt good! I had hit him so hard he fell backwards and landed on his back. His look told me he couldn't believe I had just done that to him."

Amanda shouted, "Jason, you've just made it worse for me. You'd better go, GO!"

Walking backwards and looking at them both as I departed, a sad feeling came over me as though someone had put a cloak on me that was weighing me down. The feeling was making me sick, I was feeling sick not just for Amanda, but for Gareth too.

I asked myself the questions, "if the result of their upbringing had brought them to this place in their lives, what future do they have together? Could it have been different if their fathers were around?"

It was now very clear that I had lost my childhood sweetheart. Amanda's heart was now truly taken in by Gareth, surely it was time for me to throw in the towel.

40

◼ It's Over

The fear that had overwhelmed me previously had tightened its grip? Would Amanda's story end well, or had Amanda sealed her fate by choosing to survive with men rather than to dwell in the presence of God?

On a fine spring morning, on my second trip to Manchester, I finally got my answer.

I had travelled down to Manchester to pay Amanda a visit. I was staying in a hotel and thought I would take it easy for the first day of my trip and arrange to see her on the following day. As I sat on the bed watching TV, I decided to call her and as usual she didn't pick up. Throughout the evening, I continued my efforts to get in touch but never received an answer. I decided to leave it as I was due to see her the next day anyway.

In the morning, I travelled to the hostel and made enquiries about Amanda. I'd bought clothes and food for her, I made a decision a while ago, not to give her money; I knew exactly where she was spending it and what she would spend it on.

On making my enquiries, the receptionist told me that Amanda had left the hostel the night before and hadn't returned. Hearing this, I decided to go back to my hotel and relax a bit before trying to call her again. It must have been about a day or two later, that I started having this niggling feeling, as though something was wrong. No matter how I tried to shake it off, it just wouldn't go away, maybe I would feel better if I went for a walk.

As I left the hotel and started walking towards the coffee shop, I was drawn towards a newspaper stand so I grabbed a newspaper and paid for a copy of the latest edition. I thought to myself that I would read it while drinking my coffee. I sat down, after being served by a barista, and started to read.

Being from London, I was quite intrigued with some of the news articles I was reading. The same antics that happened in London appeared to happen in Manchester as well. I don't know what made me think the two cities would be anything different from each other, but it was making quite an interesting read.

As I continued to read the paper, I gravitated toward a small column at the foot of one of the pages. There was a report about a body being found on a refuse heap. The woman had been identified as someone named Amanda. She was described as the partner of a local unemployed man. The cause of death was listed as knife wounds, evidently, she had been mercilessly stabbed to death, there was no mention of Gareth.

My body went numb, surely this couldn't be true! Without even finishing my coffee, I ran out of the shop towards the hostel. With tears filling my eyes, I kept telling myself, "No! No! This can't be true." As I got to the hostel door, I saw the police were already there—both inside and outside the building, the police were not letting anyone in. Frantically, I asked an officer what was happening and to my surprise his only response was to say, "stand aside sir."

Confused, I did as I was told and stood back, it was then I saw Gareth, handcuffed, being escorted out of the building, by two officers; my blood boiled. I screamed, "what have you done, you piece of garbage?" Before I'd realized it, I had lunged towards him and punched him square in the face, spitting out blood, he laughed and said, "she's gone mate, if I can't have her, no-one else will."

"Aargh!" I screamed out through clenched teeth as I was jostled to the ground, I too was being handcuffed. To this day the sound of Gareth's croaky voice telling me, "she's gone mate gone" is like a recurring nightmare. It was part of aa dark barren place I visit each night as I lay my head to rest.

Sad but so true, my soulmate, whose only desire in life was to be loved, was now gone. Weeks later, as I sat in church absentmindedly thinking about Amanda, a voice from deep within whispered, *you've done your best at love, you've showed the kindness of Christ even when you were being hurt and abused; there's nothing more any human being can do.*

It was as though I had awakened from a dream. I was completely aware of my surroundings, as though a fog had lifted. Just then my eye caught a glimpse of the minister. He seemed to be looking directly at me as he quoted from the Bible:

Be on your guard; stand firm in the faith; be courageous; be strong.

That's when I was sure it was time to go on with my life…

ABOUT THE AUTHOR

Lance Jones has always dreamed of writing books and has always said that one day he would get around to doing it. Well I am proud to say that several years later, he has completed his fourth book.

"She went Looking for Love", has been a journey for him, and is described as a must read book that will take you on an emotional roller coaster journey, that I am sure you're going to love it.

Lance particularly enjoys writing children's books and is creating quite a name for himself with his "The World of Taye Tari" series.

With the impact that Lance is having, I am confident that we will hear a lot more from him in the years to come.

Stephen Jones.

To Jade and
Hurrane

Enjoy

Lightning Source UK Ltd.
Milton Keynes UK
UKHW021104230420
362109UK00005B/78

9 781999 316419